Eva's World

A real woman's life

Ella Marques

Coral Orchid Press
North Miami FL

Eva's World

Disclaimer

This book is based on some realities and places I have traveled and experienced, but it is a work of fiction and any relation to real existing people is purely coincidental.

Although the author and publisher have made every effort to ensure that the information in this book was correct at press time, the author and publisher do not assume and hereby disclaim any liability to any party for any loss, damage, or disruption caused by errors or omissions, whether such errors or omissions result from negligence, accident, or any other cause.

Graphics from Bianca Cutait

Proofreading and technical support by Hatch Editorial Services. www.hatch-books.com

Coral Orchid Press, North Miami, FL

Printed in the USA

ISBN-13: 978-0-9987029-8-8 Paperback

ISBN-13: 978-0-9987029-9-5 E-Book

Visit us at www.ellamarques.com.

Contents

Eva's World is the story of a woman, a transgender, pansexual, hard-working woman, who travels the world for business and pleasure. She and her three friends, Linda, Olympia, and Victoria, come together all the time to talk about their lives, their loves, and their expectations. Two of these four women are transgender, the other two are cis women; their lives and expectations are similar, with just some small differences. This is a positive book about life as a very privileged transgender person, about traveling, about fun and expectations, but above all about love. Yes, transgender women are women. They live, they love, and they can be quite normal.

Love for a transgender person can be very complicated. Acceptance is not a given. Sometimes relationships can go very wrong for transgender people. This book shares the hope that acceptance increases and that people will realize "it's about hearts, not parts."

This story has some strong biographical aspects for the writer, but it is essentially a novel about the life of a transgender woman. Yes, we are normal people, and we want to have normal lives and be respected.

Hi, Girls

It was a cold, snowy day in Switzerland, and Eva left her house in Reinach to have lunch with her best friends, Linda, Olympia, and Victoria. They were all around the same age, between thirty-eight and forty-two years old. She was driving around to find a parking place near the old town of Basel near the Aeschengrabe. By luck she found a parking place for her black Mercedes and walked into the upscale Asian restaurant.

"Hi, I am looking for the reservation under Eva M," she told the hostess.

The hostess found her reservation and led her to the table, where Linda and Victoria were already sitting.

"Hi, sisters," said Eva. They both got up and kissed her hello.

"Hi, Eva. How are you doing?" said Victoria. "Hopefully not in too much pain."

"Give me a hug, hon," said Linda. "Welcome to womanhood, sister; you look great."

"How are you doing? I missed you both so much," said Eva as she hugged her friends. They slowly sat down.

"Where is Olympia?" she asked.

"She just texted, she is trying to find a parking space. Well, we are in Basel, it's not made for cars," said Victoria. "Yes, you really look great. I cannot believe that you had your surgery and all just a few weeks ago. You have to tell us everything."

"Yes, we are so proud of you! You are so brave. Please, tell us about everything," said Linda.

Eva was just about to launch in when she looked up and saw Olympia walking through the door. "Oh, look who is here! Olympia finally found a parking space."

They all hugged and kissed Olympia and finally sat down.

"Oh, there is a lot to catch up on, girls," said Victoria.

"Oh yes, we all have experienced a lot since we were together last time, but let's hold hands and get our energy going, enjoy each other," said Linda. They all held each other's hands, like in a chain, closed their eyes, and all took a deep breath of air. All for of them were great friends in secondary school, then two were boys and two were girls, but for many years Olympia and Linda helped Victoria ans Eva to transition and they became really very good friends. So one day they decided to come together on a regular basis, and follow each other's lives. They were really very good friend, for life.

"Sorry to disturb you girls," said the waitress, interrupting the flow of energy. "Here are the menus. Anything to drink in advance? Or shall I come back?"

"Sure, give us a minute," said Victoria as they all opened their eyes, looked at each other, and slowly got back to being in the restaurant.

"Let's have some cold sake. I am sure they have some very nice ones," said Eva. "Do you want to have an assorted sushi plate as a starter?"

"Yes," answered all the girls almost at the same time.

"Eva, tell us about your big change." Victoria gave her a gentle nudge. "I am still so jealous. I hope my time will come very soon."

"Oh my God, sisters, where shall I start? Well, from the beginning, so I flew down to Thailand. The personnel from the doctor came to get me from the airport and put me in a great hotel. I had some four days of preparation. The first two days I enjoyed a bit of Bangkok, the river markets, the great food, and mostly the temples. Mainly the Buddhist temple. It was beautiful, full of fantastic golden statues, you have to come and see it."

At just that moment the waitress came over again and asked, "Did you girls decide on something? Or shall I come a bit later?"

They put in their orders, and she left again. "Thank you," said Eva and carried on. "Well, the day for the final preparation arrived. I could only have a liquid diet and medicine to get my bowels empty. Then I was picked up in the morning from the hotel and went to the clinic. They gave me some medicine and put me in a special room next to the operation room. I was thinking of our Farewell, Penis party; it was so much fun, and soon would be a reality, what I had dreamed and hoped for all my life. Soon I would wake with a vagina. After a couple of hours they transferred me to the operation room, gave me anesthesia, and I was gone. Sometime later, I woke up back in the preparation room. Well, the surgery was done, I had a vagina, the last trace of any masculinity had irrevocably gone."

"Oh my god, girl, I cannot imagine," said Linda. "What about the pain? How long was the surgery? It's crazy how something that for us cis women is so self-evident, there from the start, is a major event for you!"

"Well, apparently the surgery lasted about seven hours," Eva explained. "The first day I didn't have much pain, the anesthesia was still in effect, but the next day, that was another story. They tried to give me some opioids, but my body reacted badly to it. The pain was really bad and the only painkiller I had was an over-the-counter medicine. The recuperation went very well, though. Soon I could walk again and do all the normal things within a couple of days. I had a catheter to help with pissing, so that was taken out, and slowly I felt like a human being again, one with a big, important difference: what I had between my legs was finally what my brain expected."

"Wow, I cannot imagine. Such a change, and the way you talk is like it was not a big deal," said Olympia.

"And I am so jealous. One of these days it will be my turn, but I still feel very scared of it. I just have to wait until a feel comfortable with it," said Victoria.

"Well, girl, there is a time for everything, and it all comes at the right time, when it is supposed to. Don't worry," said Eva.

"I have the most terrible question: What about sex? Have you already tried your new tool?" asked Linda with a smirk.

"Oh, we are very nosy, ah?" said Eva with a friendly smile. "I could not imagine you wouldn't ask that question. Well, it is still healing and I am having some training to make sure that the shape and dimensions are right, so no sex for now. It would be still too painful, and I have full sensitivity."

"Wow, sister, we really are with you and support you," said Linda. The others nodded in agreement. In the meantime the waitress came with the sushi and the drinks, so all the girls got ready to eat, drink, and of course talk.

"Linda, I heard you have a new boyfriend. When are we going to meet him?" said Eva.

"Oh, news travels fast! Yes, Frank is a real macho type, sometimes a bit much, but he is sweet, and you know I like real men. We have been going out now for about a month. He is a real bon vivant, so we like to go to good restaurants, bars, and discos. It has been quite interesting, and he is such a gentleman, I feel very reassured," said Linda.

"Oh, so nice to hear. Where did you find him? I am having so much trouble finding a decent man," said Olympia, "but I have been so busy with my work. They are always asking for more and more; eventually I may have to look for another job. Maybe create my own firm." Olympia was a lawyer; she worked for a large pharmaceuticals company in Basel.

"Well, I was invited to the wedding of an old school colleague," Linda explained, "and there Frank was, a very charming, a bit macho, but quite attractive guy. I think it was love at the first sight. We sat and drank together; from the beginning there were so many things to talk about. After the wedding, he invited me for dinner, and we had a lovely time together. He is so sexy and good in bed. Anyway we plan to keep seeing each other."

"Most men our age that look good are already married, that is the issue," said Olympia, laughing, and all the girls agreed.

"Well, you think that you have issues getting Mr. Nice Guy?" Victoria said. "For a trans person to find the right partner is very difficult. Not only do you have all the usual trouble finding the right person, but then you have to explain that you are not a woman like the others. It is really an issue."

"I certainly know what you are talking about, sister," said Eva. "I am not sure if men find me attractive at all. For a long time I had some chasers, men that particularly like transgender women, but I don't think I am interesting to them anymore because the little thing between my legs has gone. I wonder if a man would notice that I am transgender now after my surgery. Well, one thing is for sure: if the relationship goes on long enough, I would still have to tell him I was born a man."

The others nodded in thought.

"By the way, what do you think about this restaurant? The sushi is just first class, I love it," said Victoria.

"And the sake as well. I think I am starting to feel it in my head, so sweet and nice," said Linda.

9

"We should plan a trip to Japan and enjoy some sushi there," said Olympia.

"Well, Japanese sushi is very different from what we get here, very classical but very good as well," Eva said. "I think the best sushi I have ever had was either in São Paulo or in the US. They have some local varieties that Japan does not because it is more traditional. But in China it can be very good too."

"The world has become a truly global place. You can eat all different types of food all over the world. Incredible," said Olympia.

"Yes, ma'am," Linda agreed. "I have to go. I really enjoyed lunch, and I thought it was the right amount of food, even if we did not have a main course."

The girls paid and all went on with their days. They promised to contact each other over the week, mainly in their group chat.

Eva went back to her car and drove to the office near the train station in a part of town called Gundeldingen. She was a nice looking thirtyish years old girl, average height, slim with white Latin complexion, long brown hair and brown eyes, one could see the Portuguese origins. She studied engineer and was working in global business development, which had her traveling all over the world. Many years before she transitioned, she had lost her job, but then she had help from some friends and got this job. After all her papers were now OK, though that had not been without a lot of issues. Her gender confirmation surgery had been part of the deal to stay in the job and have her papers.

Switzerland usually requires gender confirmation to change a person's gender on their birth certificate, but thanks to her original Portuguese nationality, Eva had been able to change her passport and ID before the surgery. Eva was a successful professional with some experience in the trade and some international contacts in many countries. There were some places that she was not willing to travel, though, like most Islamic countries, where being trans is extremely dangerous.

Basel is a wonderful city in Switzerland, because of its fantastic medieval architecture and its history, it was a trade center for many centuries. The old Basel families are rich and very discreet, Basler people do not like to show their wealth, it's a taboo that Basel respects. Some very well known and rich families in Basel don't even put their family names on the doorbells, just their first name. Basel is a city that has borders with France and Germany. In the French side there is Alsace, a part of Europe that underwent so many wars and changed nationalities between France and Germany so many times that speaks both languages, and even have a dialect that is very near the swiss German. There is something called the three-country corner, in one point where all three countries touch each other. For many years, the Basel area had the biggest concentration of three-star Michelin chefs. The very famous restaurant guide surely spent a long time in the region.

Eva drove her Mercedes into the garage, parked, and took the elevator to the fifth floor, where her office was.

"Hi, Eva, where have you been, girl?" said Thomas, her boss.

"Hi, Thomas, I was having lunch with the girls, you know them."

"Good. Well, I'm glad that you're back. We have an issue, and I hope you can help me."

"Sure, of course. Shoot."

"Get your computer and come to my office and let's talk."

Eva grabbed her computer and her notebook and walked to Thomas's office. He was already sitting behind his desk, with a lot of paper piled up around him. He looked very cross.

"We are having problems in the office in Paris," said Thomas. "I got some messages from our accounting people that something does not match. Sales have dropped, but somehow the expenses have gone up. They don't know where some of the money is going, and they asked for help. They think that Jean Pierre is doing something that is not correct."

"Oh, they contacted you directly?" said Eva.

"Yes, I have a spy there that always let me know if there are any unusual things going on, but mostly it is a ten-minute chat about how everything is fine, and then it is over."

"I see." She leveled her boss with a glare. "Do you have a spy for me as well?"

"Eva, come on, don't be like that. You know Jean Pierre; sometimes he makes mistakes. We already talked about it."

"Just joking. So what do you want me to do?" asked Eva.

"Here, first let's study these documents, and then let's call him to establish next steps. Don't forget that he does not know what we know, so we want him to tell what is going on." Thomas shared some documents with Eva. Most were sales figures, but one was about a cash transaction for which it was not very clear who had received it.

"Oh, you are suspicious about this? I am sure he can explain it. I mean, it is a lot of money and he would not be so stupid—that is, if he wants to keep his position in the company."

"The other matter for the call is the downturn of sales, there not enough salaes ," said Thomas. "OK, let's call him and see what is going on. You call him and ask about sales, but don't tell him I am here."

Eva took out her mobile phone and dialed Jean Pierre. *"Salut, Jean Pierre."*

"Salut, Eva. Comment vas-tu?"

"I am doing great, back in Switzerland and trying to get things organized again. Had some nice time on my holidays."

"Nice to hear," said Jean Pierre. "I have some news for you, but don't tell anybody yet, especially not Thomas."

"Oh," said Eva, looking at Thomas. He nodded and motioned for her to go on. "What is going on then?"

"Look, it has been a nice time working with Thunder, but I am leaving the company. I am not earning enough, have better options, and I am leaving now."

"That is some news! So, when are you going to tell Thomas?"

"He will receive an email in half an hour or so with my resignation."

"I know that you were not doing very well with sales, but this is a big step for you. Do you have already an alternate job?"

"Yes, I do, but I cannot tell you anything. I will contact you in a couple of weeks, probably you can help me," said Jean Pierre.

It was not comfortable for Eva to be in the middle of this, but for her, loyalty to Thomas was most important.

"Jean Pierre," she said, "Thomas has just entered my office. I think you should tell him what you want to do, don't you think? I will pass the phone to him."

"Are you spying on me?, Wow girl I cannot believe this." Said Jean Pierre

"Hi, Jean Pierre, how are you doing? What do you want to tell me?" said Thomas.

"Well, Thomas, you will receive an email from me with a copy of my resignation shortly. Sorry, but this job is not for me. I have found something that suits me better."

"Oh, well, that is a surprise," said Thomas. "Well, there are some things you have to finalize even if you are leaving. I mean, you are the general manager, and you have some financial and legal matters that have to be terminated before you leave. Let me get back to you. We have to make sure that there is a proper change of hands. I will call you later today or tomorrow morning."

They ended the call.

Thomas slumped back in his chair. "Wow, I did not expect that, Eva. Sorry if you are involved. Let me think about what is going on. By the way, you do speak French, right?"

"Yes, of course."

"Let me get myself together again. I will phone you soon."

"OK, I am at your disposal." Eva stood up and walked to her office, wondering what would come next.

For the rest of the afternoon, Eva worked with her customers, making quotes, calling them, and showing them that they mattered to her. She had customers all over the world, in North and Central America, Asia, and Europe, and some of them had become very good friends. At the end of the day she drove home in Reinach, a small city on the outskirts of Basel, practically in the so-called Basel-Landschaft, meaning "the land of Basel," opposed to the city of Basel itself.

She came home. It was a nice house, but she had it all to herself. She cooked something not so exciting and opened a bottle of wine. She turned on the television, but it was too late to see the news, so she just started the next evening program.

All of a sudden there was a text on her phone from Thomas. "Talk?" he asked.

She answered, "Sure."

"Sorry to disturb you at this time, Eva," said Thomas after she took his call. "I would like to ask you a couple of things. First, can you come on Monday with me to Paris?"

"Sure, I am free. I have no planned trips so far next week."

"Great. Also, can you stay in Paris for a while until we find someone to replace Jean Pierre? I am not sure how long, but it would be great if you could interview and arrange for someone to replace him."

"Wow, that is a very heavy question. I will have to see if it is possible. I mean, I am quite surprised."

"Well, you have a lot going for you: you know French, you know our trade and a lot of people in France, you can network, so you are the ideal person to find someone in France. And you know Swiss-German people don't like to speak French." He laughed.

"OK, I get the drill; you want me to help you. No problem, Thomas. You know I am single and some time in Paris cannot be that bad for a girl like me."

"OK, I will organize the trip tomorrow. Get a hotel for the week in Paris. We will fly there on Monday morning."

"Okeydokey, sir," said Eva, a kind of confirmation phrase she used "Talk to you tomorrow."

That night she texted her group chat: "Wow, many things happened today in the office. I have to go to Paris next Monday. Not sure how long I will stay there."

The girls responded:

"Oh sister, take care! I will come to help you if you need. ⏃, anytime."

"Take care, French guys are very macho. I hope you can survive..."

"Be careful, sister, trans women are not very welcome in France."

The next morning, the trip to Paris was arranged, the hotels organized, and all was set to go. Eva was grateful to have time to get organized over the weekend. She needed to shop and get the right clothes for Paris. After all, she did not know how long she was going to stay.

A New Life in France

The weekend was over, Monday arrived, and Eva had to get up to get to the airport. If you have a six a.m. flight you always have to get up very early, meaning about three a.m., but if you are a post-op transgender girl and have to do your dilating routines, you have to add another hour, meaning waking up at 2 a.m. to catch the plane. You can always sleep on the plane, but from Basel to Paris the flight is only about an hour.

Thomas and Eva arrived at Charles de Gaulle around seven thirty. They picked up Eva's bag, rented a car, and headed to the French offices of Thunder on the outskirts of Paris, in the industrial zone of a town called Argenteuil. After a good hour of driving they arrived in front of the French HQ, parked the car, and rang the doorbell. There was a total silence, partly because they had gotten there very early, partly because they were very nervous about the outcome of the day.

"Bonjour," said Sylvie, the office manager, as she opened the door. "Oh, *mais quelle surprise*! Thomas et Eva."

"Hi Sylvie, how are you?" said Thomas as he entered the building. "Is Jean Pierre already in?"

"Yes, he just arrived. He is in his office."

Jean Pierre's office was quite spacious, with a standard desk, a lot of archiving shelves, a big meeting table, and about six chairs.

"Bonjour, Jean Pierre," said Eva as she entered the office. Thomas was already shaking hands. They all sat.

"So did you had a nice trip? I am sure you got up really early," said Jean Pierre. "And then the traffic of Paris, not easy."

"Yes, sir, and all because of you," said Thomas. "Let's discuss all the issues. Sylvie, can you get us some coffee?"

"Sure, Thomas, it's coming in a minute."

Thomas started in not such a friendly tone. "OK, what is going on? Why are you leaving? Please share all the details now."

"OK, OK," said Jean Pierre. "As you know I have been working for this company for about three years, but in the last month things have not gone very well. Somehow our customers are having problems with the testing machines. I have no feedback for most issues from the technical department, and the result is that I have no motivation anymore. Then I was approached by the competition, and they are offering me a good job. I don't want to carry on with your people."

"OK, that much is clear. I have been receiving a lot of complaints about you from the technical department. They say you do not understand anything and that you do not take their advice; it is going from bad to worse. I believe you guys have a real communication issue. Then I have these reports from the accounting people that you are spending too much money and that you took a large sum of money from the bank. Please explain."

"Oh, you mean the money from my bonus? Yes, I took it in cash to make sure that there were no issues. This money is part of my wages. It is rightly mine, Thomas."

"Prove it to me. Apparently our accountant was not informed or what?" said Thomas.

"OK, let me get Elise, our HR manager; she will explain." Jean Pierre opened the door and asked Sylvie to search for Elise.

"*Oui, oui, et le café*," said Sylvie.

"I trust you are doing your things correctly and you have everything correctly accounted for," Thomas said as the door closed. "So let's talk with Elise. The other subject is of course you leaving the company. Since French law is quite difficult in these cases, we have to make sure that we have the right papers drawn up by a lawyer, and that we sign them before we leave."

"Sure, we can do that. I suppose Eva is going to replace me here?" said Jean Pierre.

"Eva is here to help me since her French is better than mine. What happens after you leave is none of your business."

"Oh. Sorry I asked," said Jean Pierre.

The room was very chilly indeed.

At that moment the door opened and Elise arrived.

"Hi Elise, how are you?" said Thomas. "Jean Pierre is going to leave our company, and we have some urgent business to attend to."

"Bonjour, Thomas," Elise said with an apologetic squint. "Sorry for my bad English—please do not speak too fast."

"Eva can translate if necessary," said Thomas by way of assuaging Elise's concerns. "There are some things we have to look at and try to understand before Jean Pierre leaves. First there was a cash payment that was done last week, and we want to understand this."

At that moment Sylvie came in and put the coffee service in the middle of the table.

Elise grabbed a cup. "*En effet*, Jean Pierre had some money from the commission. I thought you would ask for this, so I brought his dossier. Let me look..." She searched for some pieces of paper in the thick binder. "Here is the confirmation of the commission." She opened the binder and handed a piece of paper to Thomas. He looked at it in detail, then gave the paper back to Elise.

"OK I get that this is something that was due to Jean Pierre, but I still think it is very unusual to pay such amounts with a cash withdrawal. Usually, you make a money transfer, nobody pays employees with cash anymore. Very unusual."

"Yes, I know. I told Jean Pierre as well that it was not really regular to do it," said Elise.

"OK, but now we have to do something else. Jean Pierre is going to leave the company. Can you please let us know how much we owe him?"

"Oh, that is something else. You know he has a notice period of three months in his contract, if I remember correctly, so you have to make an official notice of termination, send it to him in writing, and in three months all will be finished. I will have to calculate the amount owed."

"So let's make sure I understand. Jean Pierre is going to stop working this morning. I will call my lawyer, that is a specialist in French personnel matters; we will draft a paper of understanding for the termination of the contract, we will all sign it, and by this afternoon all will be finished," Thomas said. Jean Pierre's mouth and eyes were wide open. "Eva, can you go with Elise and help her with the calculations?" French employment law is very protective for employees, and problematic if you do something wrong, so it is usual in such cases to make a note of understanding between both parties.

"Sure, Thomas. Elise, let's go and get this done."

Eva and Elise stood up and left the room.

"Oh, this sounds like big changes are taking place," said Elise as they walked down the corridor.

"Yes, I think so. Jean Pierre is going to the competition, so Thomas wants him to leave very fast, so we have to get everything ready."

They both went to Elise's office. There were some questions, but they got the numbers right for the dismissal of Jean Pierre.

Eva went back to the management office and found a telephone conference going on, with Jean Pierre, Thomas, and what seemed to be a lawyer on the other end of the line.

"Yes, I will have the papers ready for the signature of all concerned, but I need the calculation to finalize them," said the voice on the phone.

"Eva just came in, she is helping me get it all together. Eva, do you have the dismissal costs?"

Thomas looked in detail at the numbers; he took out his phone and made some calculations as well. "It seems like a lot of money, but if that is what the French law says, then it has to be right. So I have the calculation; we are sending it to you by email in the next minutes. Eva, can you go to Sylvie, scan the paper, and send it to this email address?"

"Sure, on my way," said Eva. She went to Elise office, and they sent the email with the calculation to the lawyer. She zipped back to the management office and gave Thomas a nod.

"Mr. Dupont, Eva just sent you the calculation. Can you confirm you got it?"

"Yes, everything is here. I will reply with all the papers to sign within the next half hour."

"OK, perfect, we are getting all organized." Thomas closed the call and turned to Eva. "Can you get the list of equipment that Jean Pierre has on loaned items from the business?"

"OK I will get it" And she went to Elise's office to get the papers. When she came back all three sat in the office table. The tension was high; she could fell that there was definite mistrust in the room.

"Here you have the list, but please be nice with each other! no blood ok?" Said Eva as she came back.

Thomas looked at the list. "Jean Pierre, do you agree with the decision that we took?"

Jean Pierre shrugged. "What can I do? Thank you for being generous in your approach. I can understand that you are not happy that I am going to the competition, and I'm sorry that I took the money in cash, that was not so nice. I will sign your papers and will see you sometime in an exhibition or god knows where."

"OK, now, according to this list, you have to give us the car. Do you want Eva to drive you somewhere?"

"No, no, I will take a taxi."

"And of course we'll need the phone, the computer. Please tell us your password to your computer and to your business email. The private ones you can send somewhere else or delete."

He rapped the table twice with the sheaf of papers. "So now let's have a small discussion about your important business and daily schedule. You have to discuss them with Eva. She will be replacing you until we have someone for your permanent role."

Soon, Sylvie knocked at the door and came in with some ten pages of paper, which Jean Pierre and Thomas signed.

"OK, time to go," said Jean Pierre. "*Vous ne faites pas dans la dentelle*, that is for sure. I never imagined that you would literally throw me out of the company so fast. Anyway, see you around. Eva, enjoy France." He asked Sylvie to order a taxi and was gone.

With Jean Pierre gone, the tension all of a sudden was gone.

"I never expected this morning to be like that. Learned a lot from you." Said Eva with some sense of relief.

"OK, Eva, you get organized here in France," Thomas said. "Let's see in the next weeks how it goes and we'll either make you GM of France or you will be *ad interim* until we find someone. I think the first thing to do is inform all customers and visit the most important ones. But now let's go for lunch and then you can drive me to the airport."

"Wow, I have some thinking to do. I mean, sure, I do not have a spouse and am very flexible, but I will send you the bill," Eva said with a laugh.

Thomas looked tired but smiled indulgently at her joke. "Sure, but hey, I am hungry. Let's go."

Sylvie, Thomas, and Eva drove to Courtepaille, a nearby popular chain restaurant, something classical but quite good.

"Now you have to tell me who my boss is," Sylvie told Thomas after they all sat down at a small, round table.

"Eva is now your boss, until we decide what is next."

"May I ask you why Jean Pierre left?"

Thomas sighed. "Well, Sylvie, I think he was more worried about his own goals than the company's goals, and somehow they were not compatible. He is leaving now for the competition, so I ask you to be very careful if he phones or wants to have any kind of information from you. When in doubt, please contact Eva or myself. Anyway, what can you tell us about him?"

"Well, with me he was always proper, but I noticed that lately he was somehow a bit far away from the business. I thought he was having issues at home with his wife or something."

"Apparently he was dealing with the competition," said Eva tartly.

"So what are you girls going to eat?" asked Thomas as the waitress approached the table for the order.

"I just want to have a bavette with green beans instead of fries, and a water," said Sylvie.

"It has been a while since I was in France," said Eva. "I would like to have a tartare with French fries; I cannot resist. And some water, I still have to drive."

"I am going to have a confit de canard with French fries. Sometimes you need some comfort food. And I am going to have a glass of red wine," said Thomas.

Lunch was certainly not so difficult and heavy an affair as that morning had been. The three talked about family, hobbies, friends, and holidays. After lunch, Eva drove Thomas to the airport and took a taxi back to the office. As Jean Pierre's replacement she would take over the company car, a nice, new Peugeot. It had been a long day, so she clocked out early and drove to the hotel quite early. She had a short rest and something small to eat in a restaurant next door. She texted her friends that she was in Paris but didn't know for how long. It was an early night, after her early morning.

Eva was staying at a Mercure Hotel, a well-known French chain. It was not a cheap, but it was certainly good. She got up early, had a good breakfast, and went to the office.

"Hi, Sylvie, have you recovered from yesterday's shock?" said Eva.

"I could not sleep very well," Sylvie admitted, "but I think things will go back to normal soon."

"OK." Eva smiled. "Let me get organized in my new office, but then we have to make a letter for all our customers about the changes in the company, that is first priority. I have to make some extra phone calls as well because I still have my own customers all over the world, and they have to know what is going on."

Sylvie nodded and got right to work.

Eva walked into Jean Pierre's old office—hers now—and hung up her coat behind the door. "Morning, Thomas," she said once she connected with him over the phone. "How are you? Did you had a safe trip back? Did you rest?"

"Yes, yes, yes," answered Thomas. "All good, but there's a lot of work to do. We have to send a letter to the customers, then we have to find someone to be the future GM of France, and of course don't forget your customers as well, mainly the company in Bangalore."

"Oh, Thomas, you're right as always. As far as the letter to customers is concerned, I have sent you a draft for your approval. Sylvie is gathering the email addresses to send all the emails by this afternoon. Pleas look at it and get back to me. I will send a little letter to all my direct customers worldwide today, and will phone the most important ones. As for recruiting"—she scratched her head—"please help, I have no clue."

"I will have to speak with our HR guru here in Switzerland. I don't want to involve the local French HR, they are not specialized in this type of work. In the meantime, please try to find some kind of apartment for yourself, somewhere where you can be at ease and happy, ideally an already furnished place. We will pay for everything for the next six months; then we will have to see what happens."

"OK, that sounds like a plan. Anything else to discuss?"

"Yes. With your customers, you do what you have to do. I will get our finance department to get you an unlimited credit card, I think you will need it. For your trips, please use our people here in Switzerland. After all, you remain a Swiss employee."

"Wow, now I know why you are the boss," Eva said. "You know how to deal with things."

With Thomas's approval, Eva sent the email to the customers of the French subsidiary some hours later. Then she worked on her own customers, telling them what happened and that she would still be working with them, though probably not so intense as in the last weeks.

At the end of the day she was exhausted; it was time to tell the girls about what is happening. They all made time for a conference call.

"Hi, girls," said Eva. "You will never believe what has happened since I've been here in Paris."

"Yes, girl, tell us all about it! Stop the suspense," said Olympia.

"Well, I had two very exhausting days. Yesterday I got to Paris very early with my boss, Thomas. We sent the old managing director for France out of the company; that was very intense. Today I am the new managing director for France, I don't know for how long, and am getting all organized. Girls, I am getting an apartment here in Paris! You all have to come and visit me. In the meantime, I will go to Basel most weekends, and do my usual trips, though I don't know how."

"Wow, girl, that is a big change," said Linda. "Congrats! You rock."

"I cannot believe that my sister is such a hit. My God, that's incredible," said Victoria. "We will have to come and test the men in Paris together. I will come soon."

That got a laugh from the group.

What a telephone conference! It was really nice to have some feedback from her best friends, but really, Eva was a bit lost. It was the peak of a new experience, but she was also alone in a new, huge city. She couldn't complain about that, though. What a city! The incredible culture, the food, the wine, the museums, it was all the best in the world. It would probably take ten years to know everything about Paris; they say that it will take two lifetimes to try all the restaurants, so it was clear to Eva that she would have to organize herself to try all the good things in six months. Yes this time she would be living here, for once she was not limited by time as a tourists or a business traveler, a big, big difference.

That evening, Eva decided to take a small tour of the city, to go and see some of the iconic places from the outside, some of the places that she already knew and that meant a lot to her.

Though it was late, the traffic she drove through was still heavy. She went down from her hotel in Argenteuil to Asnières-sur-Seine, Clichy, and went to the top of the Sacre Coeur. She managed to park the car and walk there.

What a gorgeous view over Paris. Through the wonderful lights, she could spot the Louvre, the Tour Eifel, Montparnasse; it was such a gorgeous place. Then she scored a table at one of the most iconic restaurants in Paris, La Mère Catherine, a place that she had visited many times over. She had come to realize it had the best *soupe à l'oignon* in the world. During dinner she was thinking how lucky she was, her acceptance after the transition had been so big, never had a really issue, but mostly felling her real self made such a difference.

After dinner she ping-ponged around the city. She drove to the Boulevard de Clichy, down to the Bastille, to Notre Dame de Paris, then in the direction of the Tour Montparnasse, and then to Champs de Mars and Tour Eifel, a very special monument. From there she went to the Musée de l'Homme, then to the Tuileries until the Louvre, only to turn back at the Place de la Concorde. She went up les Champs Elysées and arrived at the most iconic roundabout in the world, the Arc de Triomphe. Typically that roundabout made you prove your driving prowess, but that night, there was not as much traffic as usual. Finally, Eva went slowly home through the Bois de Boulogne, Nanterre, and Argenteuil.

When she entered the Bois de Bologne Eva could not stop from feeling emotional. She saw the transgender and crossdressing prostitutes, hundreds of girls trying to get men to stop their cars and buy what they were selling. The Bois was many things, but it was a terrible place where transgender people got raped, even killed, daily. Since the eighties it had been a magnet for many terrible things. At one time the prostitutes were called *les brésiliennes*, because apparently it was the largest export from Brazil: perfect girls that had a penis between their legs. For many it was the only way to survive, and Eva felt torn between pity and a guilty feeling of luck that she could have a career and did not have to go through that. There was a time she would have done it, though, just to be a girl. Not many people understood what it meant to be transgender, in her experience. It is more than anything that you experience in life; it is not a choice.

At the end of her first full day, she was exhausted but very happy. Paris, gay Paris, beautiful Paris, whatever you call that place, it was going to be her home for some time.

The next morning she woke up, looked at her emails, and drove to the office. There was always an issue with parking the car; that was one of the worst things about that beautiful city. Even so, Eva was determined to find the best places to see and to go to the theater at least twice a week, take advantage of the fact that she was in such an iconic cultural place.

She arrived at the office; started to work, mainly on seeing what to do with her own customers; met the French crew; organized an informative meeting with her people; and tried to get the first French customer visits organized.

Just before lunch, Sylvie rushed into Eva's office and said, "I have Mr. Mani from Monaco on the line; he wants to talk with you."

"Who is he?"

"He is the richest man in Monaco. He has a company called Mecaplast, heavy money, and a lot of power," said Bouron, the technical manager of the French operation.

"Oh, what does he want? Do you know?" asked Eva.

"Well, I think he has a court case with us. Jean Pierre told me that but no details."

"OK, let's see." Eva rolled her shoulders, got in the zone, and took the phone call.

"Bonjour, Mr. Mani," said Eva. "How can I help you?"

"Hello, Miss Eva, I don't know if you can help me, but for sure I can help you."

"That sounds very promising, I am sure you are going to tell me all about it."

"Sure. My lawyers are going to contact you shortly. Did Jean Pierre tell you what was going on?"

Eva was taken aback by this gentleman's informality. "You seem to be very well informed about everything, my compliments, but I have to say, I don't really know what you are talking about."

"Does not surprise me, he did not really tell anybody," said Charles Mani. "My proposition is very simple: my lawyers will send you all the information and next week you will come to Monaco and we discuss the details. My secretary will organize the dates with you. It was really nice to talk with you, and I hope to see you next week."

"OK, that sounds reasonable. I will contact your secretary." Eva immediately called Thomas. "Hi, boss, I just had an incredible telephone conversation with a Mr. Charles Mani from Monaco. Do you know him?"

"No, I don't, but Jean Pierre told me before he left that there was a legal issue with a very big company in Monaco. It must have been that. Find out what is going on and let's see what we can do," said Thomas.

It only took a couple of days, and all the information came from the lawyers. Essentially, Mecaplast wanted to file a lawsuit with Thunder for what they described as a defective machine that was delivered. To Eva, it looked like someone had no clue what they were doing; the issue, though, was that the employee lost an arm in the process. All the information was transmitted to headquarters, and Thunder got their lawyers on the information channel. Eva contacted Mani's secretary, and a visit to Monaco was organized.

In the afternoon she took a flight from Orly to Nice. As she arrived, she saw that she had some people waiting for her. She walked to the heliport, entered a helicopter, and had a breathtaking trip to Monaco. On one side, there were the mountains of the south of France; on the other, the adorable

Mediterranean sea. She was not just flying over any place, but Cap Ferrat, Villefranche-sur-Mer, and Cap-d'Ail. As she looked down she saw some amazing yachts and fantastic views.

Later that evening the chauffeur picked her up and drove her to a restaurant on the side of the old port, in front of the Castel of the Prince of Monaco.

"Bonjour, Eva," said an older man. He was short, with white hair, and Eva could see the incredible energy that he brought with him. "I am Charles Mani. I thank you for coming to see me. You look astonishing."

Eva had known it was going to be an interesting evening, so she had worn a very nice, dark blue knee long figure tight dress with just enough neckline to show her jewelry but not much more.

"Hello, Mr. Mani, it is a pleasure to meet you in this incredibly beautiful place. And thank you for all the arrangements."

Mr. Mani smiled. "Well, I would like to introduce some of the people that work for me." He presented Eva to the three gentlemen that were with him, and apparently worked for him as well.

They struck up the usual conversation—where they came from, what they had done before. Mr. Mani was the real boss; he told Eva all about his history, how he became rich, his first job making the chips for the famous casino of Monaco. It was all very entertaining and incredibly interesting.

Sometime in the middle of the discussion, Mr. Mani looked at her and said, "Eva, there is a legal process going on between our companies, but I think we can be friends. You are a very pleasant person, but please do not take this personally. A lawsuit for me is like any other source of money: if there is potential, we will go ahead with it. Anyway, I really enjoyed this evening, but tomorrow we will talk more about our small differences."

The next day Mr. Mani showed her the manufacturing unit, probably the only in Monaco. They had many discussions with lawyers and manufacturing workers. At the end of the day Eva went back to Paris, thinking about all she had seen. What a trip; she was impressed. And of course she had to tell her closest friends all about it.

On the way back to Paris, Eva thought about how she had to get organized. She asked around and got an apartment in Asnières-sur-Seine—closer to Paris than Argenteuil, but not the price of Paris. Eva was traveling all over France, and she was really starting to know this amazing country. One of her favorite moments was when she was invited to one of the most incredible monuments of French cuisine, the Organ Room of Paul Bocuse in Lyon, for an event sponsored by one of her customers.

In this very big room, one wall is a working organ from the nineteenth century, full of music and movement. The rest of the room is heavily decorated as well; Eva felt as though she was in a party from the *fin de siècle*. Not only was the room incredible, but the food was the best of the best French cuisine. They had a wonderful *poulet de Bresse* with truffles and morel mushrooms. Well the Lyon area has a worldwide reputation for cuisine, with iconic restaurants like La mere Brazier, Lyon de Lion, le vieux Lyon, Brasserie le Nord not to forget the immense amount of small bouchons, local name for typical restaurants.

Yes, food in France was very regional, and one must say where there is good wine, there is good food. There was Alsace, the Lyon area including Bourgogne and Savoy, Provence, the west with Bordeaux, just to mention a few.

And of course, Paris represented all of them. Eva was dazzled by all the incredible restaurants in Paris. They say you could live your all life in Paris and have lunch and dinner at a different restaurant every day and never eat in all restaurants. Eva frequented places like la Tour d'Argent, Pied au Couchon, Jules Vernes, and of course, the restaurant that became Eva's all-time preferred restaurant, Le Grand Colbert in the rue Vivienne. The menu is traditional French, with Burgundy snails, veal kidneys, *boeuf bourgignon,* and all that in a 1920s atmosphere. This was her favorite place to meet up with business partners and friends.

Even so, she was spending most of her weekends in Basel and having great, though less glitzy, dinners with her best friends.

First Holidays in the Caribbean

It was a Sunday with Eva in Switzerland and the girls decided to have a nice brunch in Mövenpick, a great restaurant in beautiful downtown Basel, on the Marketplatz. After the usual hellos, kisses, and hugs, the four girls got their food from the buffet and sat down at the table.

"Oh my God, I've gone so long without a proper *zopf* with butter," said Eva. She bit into the braided bread, enjoying its eggy sweetness. "I am having a wild time in France, don't get me wrong, but sometimes I really miss Switzerland. Well, I miss many things around the world."

"I can understand that. Honestly, I could not be out of Switzerland for more than three weeks; I love this country," said Linda.

"Well that is your view. I would go anywhere. I am dreaming of going to live in a warm country. I don't like the snow. I would love to go to the Caribbean and be a pirate," said Olympia.

"Oh no, they would kill me around there! Can you imagine? They are very transphobic and homophobic; that would be an issue." said Victoria.

"Yes I think you are right," Eva said. "The Caribbean is very homo- and transphobic, but you pass very well. I am sure you would not have an issue. I mean your papers are updated as well, right?"

"Well, not completely," Victoria admitted. "I am still working on my passport."

"Oh my god, then it can be an issue. I would love to go for a sailing trip to the Caribbean. It would be just great; I need a holiday, believe me," said Eva. "My life in France is just incredible, though there's lots of work. I have been visiting customers all over the place, from north to south and east to west. I spend many hours in the car and a lot of time with French customers. They like me a lot, but I am getting tired, need some fresh air."

"Yes, a sailing trip in the Caribbean would be really great," said Linda. "I would probably try to get Frank to come too. We have not had a real holiday for a while."

Olympia's eyes glinted in excitement. "Yes, girls! Let's do it. Victoria, we will take care of you. Don't worry, you will be in good hands."

"No, girls, I cannot come," Victoria said. "Even if I got my passport in order, my finances are not doing well enough to afford such a trip, but please go and send me a lot of photos. I will be with you in spirit."

"If you're sure, Victoria?" Eva asked. When Victoria nodded sadly, Eva said, "Well, I can ask Fred. He is a friend of mine who is a skipper; probably he can help plan our itinerary."

The girls carried on talking about work, love, friends, and the things they had done lately. Some days later Eva wrote to them in the group chat.

"Hi, girls, just got a message from Fred. He has a Cigale 16 in Martinique, and we could go sailing there for about two weeks. We can have eight people maximum including the skipper. Depending on when, he might have a customer as well, but he is OK if we come. What do you think? The proposition is the last two weeks of February. He proposes to go from Le Marin all the way down to Grenada and back, it would be a fantastic trip. Who is in?"

"Linda and Frank are in, but we need to know the prices first."

"Olympia as well, and prices please."

"Sorry sisters, Victoria is not in, probably next time."

Soon all was arranged—flights, hotels, diving gear, protective cases for phones and wallets, but most important, gorgeous bikinis, shirts, and caps, all to be beautiful.

They got the cheapest flights with an intermediate stop on the island of St. Martin. Of course, they had to leave the airport and drink a piña colada at the Sunset Grill and watch the planes land. It was a remarkable scene because the planes are so close to the water that you can literally see the people inside the airplane when you are in the Sunset Grill.

All four of them arrived tired and happy at Fort de France, the capital of Martinique. After all formalities and introductions, they took a taxi to the private harbor of Le Marin.

Fred walked down the pier and after greeting Eva said hello to her friends. Fred was quite a looker, not too tall, tanned white skin, blue eyes, dark brownish short hair, mostly with a 3-day beard and a muscular hairy body.

"I'll be your skipper for the next two weeks." He took in both women, Frank, and their luggage. "You guys must be exhausted."

"Hi Fred, yes, we are exhausted and looking forward to having a quiet evening somehow," said Eva.

"OK, David, the last person, arrived about half an hour ago, and he is already in the boat. We have a lovely, big, sixteen-meter—or fifty-two-foot—

boat, so there will be plenty of space for everybody. I will tell you where your cabins are, we then put everything in the cabins and do a safety talk and round about the boat. Question: How many of you have done such a sailing trip already?"

Just about everybody lifted their hands in affirmation.

"Great, I have an experienced crew. We will talk more about that soon.

"After the security instructions and getting to know the boat," Fred continued, "we will sit down together and I will present the itinerary that I propose. We can always change something if you want to stay longer somewhere or skip a stop, and after our discussion, we will go out to dinner. Tomorrow morning we will go to do the shopping; we need enough food for at least one week. Since it is going to be a trip where we will be in many countries and they have some formalities, you need to give me all your passports. We will go from Martinique, that is French, to St. Lucia, and then on to St. Vincent and the Grenadines. All these countries require customs, and they are not so fast at processing them as in Europe. OK, let's go to the *Isabelle*."

The Isabelle was a very beautiful boat, and the first thing they did was find where everybody would sleep and put the right luggage in the right place.

"Hi, everybody," a man said, just as Eva was stowing her hand luggage. "My name is David, I hope you had a good trip." David was a typical swiss looking man, tall short brown hair, grey greenish eyes thin but with a slight belly, waring the typical summer sailing outfit, meaning shorts, an open shirt showing his hairy chest and brown moccasin shoes.

"Hi David, nice to meet you, hope you had a nice trip as well." they all said and added their names. They were going to be living together for two weeks, in a little nutshell, so they hoped that everyone would get along well.

Everyone was setting their own luggage in their spaces. There were four cabins and two bathrooms, so Linda and Frank were in a one-bedroom cabin, Eva and Olympia were in a cabin with bunk beds, David had one bed for him, and Fred was in a two-bedroom cabin similar to Eva and Olympia's.

"Hi guys, time for the welcomes and instructions. Please come up to the cockpit," said Fred.

All came slowly out and got comfortable for the talk.

"So, sorry, but this talk is part of the usual drill, let's get acquainted with the crew, meaning you. Let's go around, say your name, your sailing experience, what you think you can do best on a boat, and anything about yourself. Jokes are always welcome. I will start with myself. So I am Fred, I don't know if you read the CV I sent you, so I am your skipper, the boss. Just to make things clear, I take responsibility for what is going on around this boat, so I would be very happy if you follow what I ask of you, mainly anything that has to do with security and safety. I am a professional skipper; I got my Swiss permit about twenty years ago, and I have sailed in many waters, the Atlantic, Pacific, and Indian Oceans, and the Mediterranean Sea. I have been stationed here in the Caribbean now for five years, and I know this area very well. I am single, never married, I mean who would like to live with a vagabond like me? I like cooking, navigating, all things to be done in the boat. OK, questions can come later. Next, Linda."

"Yes, my name is Linda. I am here with my love, Frank. This is my third sailing trip, so I know something about sailing but am not an expert. I like trimming, cooking, swimming, and diving, good food and some booze from time to time."

"Hi, I am Frank. I am an engineer, mechanical, it's my fourth sailing experience. I did the theory for my skipper license, so please sign my log book," he joked to Skipper Fred. "I still need five hundred of the thousand miles to get my license. I like to do many things, but navigation and being helmsman are my specialties. In particular I would like to have some training on man overboard, can be a woman, too, and knots."

"My turn? OK, my name is Olympia. It's my second sailing experience. My good friends Linda and Eva always want me to come, and cooking and doing nothing are some of my expertise."

"My name is Eva, I got my skipper's license about five years ago. I have sailed with Fred twice, so we know each other, I love cooking, trimming sails, navigation, swimming, and diving."

"Nice to hear from all of you. I am David; I finished my theory exams for skipper and am trying to get the thousand miles like Frank. It's my fourth sailing trip and always with Fred."

"Great, nice to see that you all have sailing experience," said Fred/ "This is quite a standard sloop type of boat, but it is big, so more force is needed for some work. All the sailing functions come from the cockpit, so you don't usually have to do much at the base of the mast. Be careful with the boom, it is just over the cockpit so it can be dangerous..."

Fred showed them all the important things on the boat, and then everybody went downstairs to the bathrooms, where he showed them the functions; then to the captain's desk, where he showed them the function of the VHS and the water monitor. They made the complete tour of the boat.

Back in the cockpit, Fred said, "Tomorrow you guys have to go shopping for the next few weeks. I will go with you, but I would suggest you make a list of what you want. Now let's go to eat, I am sure we are all quite hungry."

Eva grabbed a piece of paper and a pen from her things, and then they all left the boat and went to one of the nearby restaurants with a view of the marina.

They had a very relaxed dinner with some booze and managed to make a kind of shopping list for the next day. Later they went back to the *Isabelle* and went to their quarters for some sleep. Not many of them slept, aside from Fred. Eva, for instance, had to get used to the movement of the boat again, as well as the noises that come from nearby boats.

The next morning everybody woke quite early, took a taxi to a nearby supermarket, and had a breakfast in a nearby coffee shop. Afterward there was a lot of shopping—water, wine, beer, meat, vegetables, fish, snacks, what a huge list! They drove back to the boat and put everything in the right place. They certainly needed some imagination to find the best fit for all they had bought.

"So we have to get some fuel and water," said Fred, "and then we will sail south to St. Vincent. Do you want to eat now, when we arrive, or have a snack on the way?"

"How long are we going to sail?" asked Linda.

"Well it will all depend on the wind. Let's go downstairs and calculate." They all walked down to the captain's table. "Mrs. Eva," the skipper said, "sit down here and please find the right chart. We are going to St Lucia."

"Sure," she said. "But why me?"

"I think you have the most experience with charts in the group."

Eva opened the table and very quickly found a chart for Martinique and St. Lucia. She put it on the table and got a compass. "So where are we going?"

"Let's go to the iconic Marigot Bay. So if we stay and eat in the boat and do not go to the island, we do not have to go through customs."

"Found it, let me see. There are about thirty-one nautical miles, so what is our speed?"

"It will depend on a lot of things, such as wind speed and direction, and how good we are at working together. We should calculate six knots, meaning about five hours. What is the weather forecast? Do you know?"

"Where is your Weather Fax? Well, it looks like we have something like a wind of fifteen knots east to northeast. That means we are in the lee part of the island, and we will only have wind in the channel, meaning in the portion between both islands."

Fred gave her a grin. "Well done, miss. Let's go."

They all went outside, and soon enough the skipper was again by Eva's side. "Eva, which mooring are we going to take first?"

Eva pretended to fan herself. "Whoo! Hard work already on the first day. OK, let me see. The wind comes from the back of the boat, so the back, meaning the stern lines, we will put them in a slip and slowly let go as the anchor is lifted."

"Well done! David, you go to the anchor; Eva, you stay in the back and do the maneuver. For the petrol station, we will need a stern and a bow line. We will let the guys work. David, you stay in front."

They all prepared the boat. It was a very good maneuver. Eva had turned on the motor, got the lines ready, and gave the signal to David that they were ready to go, and they started to move forward with the anchor winch. At the same time stability was ensured by the stern line. They left their mooring, slowly the anchor went up, David gave the sign, and they went in the direction of the petrol station with a turn to port.

The boys were getting the lines ready. Eva was going very slowly, looking to see if the petrol station was free. After a few minutes, they approached the petrol station sideways, sent both moorings to the attendant, and stopped the boat. It was an easy positioning; they were on the lee side of the island with no real wind to buffet their spot. The boat was filled with petrol. The boat treasurer was Olympia; everybody had given her money for the first days, and they were using it for food, petrol, and all other expenses.

After they were finished, they maneuvered *Isabelle* out of the bay. Eva was steering with use of the motor; as they went out of the bay they started to go southwest, with a long way to go to get to the island.

"Let's set sails, crew," said Fred. "David, you go to the mast just in case. We will do the main sail first and then the jib. Frank, you stay in the cockpit to set the mainsail." Said Fred.

Everybody moved into position. Fred showed them what they had to work with and then he said, "Eva, please move into position."

Eva reduced the speed of the boat and headed to the wind direction until the boat was in exactly the right place. The sail was lifted and, wow they were finally under sails. Then Fred started to unroll the jib. The wind really sent it flapping, so Eva started to put the boat in the exact cap to trim the sails. Wow, what a sensation! she thought. They were sailing, the motor was turned off, and there was nothing but the wind and, as the boat started to go faster, the peaceful rush of the water.

Eva gave the helm to Linda; she was doing well. They slowly moved out of the protected area, and as they came to the channel between Martinique and St. Vincent, the boat started to have a bigger heel, but all within the normal range. A little more trimming and they were going at seven knots. They were all very happy.

At that moment, Eva entered a different world, full of peace, serenity, and accomplishment. Both Linda and Olympia noticed and looked at her. Eva and Olympia left the cockpit and sat down next to each other on the port side of the boat. They could feel the energy of the moment; it was magical.

Once everything was underway, Fred sat next to Eva. "Well done, skipper," he teased her. "That was really good, I am glad you didn't forget."

"Thank you, captain," said Eva, and looked at him with an incredibly serene eye.

It took another three hours to approach the northern tip of St. Lucia, a volcanic island with fantastic mountains and lush, green surroundings.

They could see the city of Castries, and soon they came to Marigot Bay, a complete paradise. Before they entered the bay, they lowered the main sail and rolled up the jib. They were then traveling under motor and very slowly started to look for a suitable place to set anchor, somewhere where they would be protected from the winds. As soon as they found a spot, they dropped the anchor. This time Eva was dropping the anchor and Fred was steering.

"Here we are, everybody. Now we need the most important thing, the anchor slug. Kids, who is going to do it?"

Frank and David went inside the boat together, and it was not long before they came back with beers, chips, and some savory snacks.

They started to talk together, tell jokes, and have a great time. Eva was thrilled that the group she'd put together had such great chemistry.

She jumped in the beautiful, clear bay water. It was fantastic, and soon everybody was bathing in this gorgeous place. The plans were made for next day. They would enter St. Vincent and the Grenadines, so they had to go through a port of entry, and there were not many of those. They chose Wallilabou Bay, about forty-six nautical miles or between seven and nine hours away. The only issue was that customs was only open between four and six p.m., so if they arrived too late, the wait would be considerable. They decided to set sail at seven a.m.

The anchor-slug maneuver was not very difficult, and David and Fred did the whole thing while the others watched. They left the bay with the motor running and set the main sail as they got out. Well there was not much wind behind the island of St. Lucia that morning, so they decided to use the motor for about three hours. Then the wind grew stronger because the channel between the islands was approaching, so they shut down the motor, opened the jib, and were slowly taking on speed again.

The view was magnificent, the Pitons, the volcanic island mountains, were incredible. On the other side there was this feeling of emptiness—the water, the horizon, and the sky with very little clouds. Well, that was if Eva did not look in detail at the water. It was the residence of many incredible animals.

The crew was relaxing all over; they were on autopilot with David watching over. Linda was in Frank's arms in the cockpit; they were kissing each other and enjoying the gorgeous day, a day to remember. Olympia and Eva were on the starboard side of the boat sitting, with their legs leaning out. They were trying to see what was going on in the water. Sometimes they would detect a fish jumping, and sometimes, two or three dolphins would come out, look at who they were, and go back in again. A group of three dove underneath the boat, jumping out at the bow, then going back to the stern to repeat the same maneuver. The girls felt really privileged; it was like having their own zoo.

Fred sat down next to Eva, and they all were contemplating the view.

"Oh my god, look at that! At one hundred twenty degrees," Eva said.

They all looked and there was a general Ah of excitement. They were all looking at a whale jumping out of the water and falling back in with a big splash.

"Oh, is that a humpback whale?" said Olympia.

"I believe so. It's their mating season, and there are quite a lot of them around here," said Fred.

"Yes, I can see a smaller whale next to the big one," said Linda.

"Holy shit, look just next to the boat," said Eva.

"Wow, that is a big eye," said Olympia.

"Yes and he is looking at us to see what are we doing, very clever animals. Anyone up for a dive with the whale?" said Fred.

The response was unanimous: "NO! Have you seen the size of that eye? It is bigger than my face."

They all sailed south to the next island. The pirate feeling was obvious; they were in a small nutshell in the middle of the Caribbean Sea.

As they approached St. Vincent, Eva changed to the port side to have a better look at the beautiful volcanic island. Fred followed her there. They were very close to each other, and what Eva had suspected was an attraction was becoming much more evident. She was close enough to Fred to see the flecks of color in his eyes and to smell his musk, and well, that was very exciting for her.

Fred took her hand and looked her in the eyes, a look that transformed into a kiss within a couple of seconds. Eva's emergency system kicked off. On one side there was the obvious attraction, but on the other she was scared.

"What am I doing?" she wondered. "He does not know that I am trans. I have to tell him—well, I have a vagina now, so he would probably not notice anyway. What shall I do? Eva, girl, stay quiet and enjoy."

The kissing was apparently drawing some spectators. They could hear a sudden cough from the others on the boat, but that did not embarrass them, and they continued.

They finally arrived at the lovely bay of Wallilabou. They set anchor and set up the dinghy with its motor. Fred got all the boat documents and passports, and put them in a plastic waterproof bag. He and Eva went to land to do the customs work while the others stayed on the boat drinking and having some fun.

They arrived at the island, secured the dinghy, and walked to the custom center, which was not yet open. On the way they were rubbing against each other and kissing each other.

"Fred, you are just too sexy," Eva purred.

I am mad about you, Eva. You are such a special girl, you have to tell me everything about you."

"Sure, I think we will have a lot of time to catch up," said Eva between kisses. She had made a decision: she had the right to be happy and let things go as they would. *I will tell him if things get more serious*, she thought.

After they cleared customs, they went back to the boat. Everyone was waiting for them with a kind of suspicious look.

"Back already," said Linda, laughing.

"All clear now," Fred announced, as though his hair wasn't mussed and his lips weren't swollen with kisses. "We can go anywhere in St. Vincent and the Grenadines. We are officially here."

The rest of the afternoon they relaxed on the cockpit and deck.

Eva and Fred found it hard not to kiss and hug the whole time.

"So, tell me everything about yourself," said Fred.

"Well, there is a lot to say, but you already know a lot. After all it's the third time we've sailed together. You tell me about you," said Eva.

"Well, I am just a skipper, going from island to Island, and being free as a whale."

"OK." She folded her arms. "How many girls have you had in the last few months?"

"That is not a question you should ask! Of course I had some girls, but none like you."

"I can imagine, I know sailors have a different wife in every port." And she was thinking, *I am sure you never had a trans girl like me, that's for sure.*

"No, no, no, I am a serious man, believe me," said Fred.

In the evening they all took the dinghy and went to have dinner in a restaurant in the village. It was a good Caribbean dinner with conch and some delicious curry. After dinner they went back to the boat. They had a small chat and a beer, and then everyone went to bed.

Fred was waiting for Eva in front of his room. He touched her around the neck in a lovely way and said, "Are you coming in?"

Wow, that was clear and direct, and she was just as ready. She told him she would be in his room in a minute, then she went to her room, went to the restroom, had a very short dilation session to open up her vagina and get some lubricant inside. As a transgender the natural lubrification is not so high as with most cis women, so you always have to put some gel in it, as for the dilation, it takes a long time until the newly made vagina is not swollen anymore, during this time it is better to do this before sex, anyway everybody is slightly different. It would be the first time that she used her new tool, and she was very nervous, mainly she was scared that his tool would be too big and not fit in properly and it would be painful. As she passed back through her room, she said to Olympia, "Sorry, girl, sleeping next door," and went to the other cabin.

What happened there was just incredible. He kissed her deeply on her mouth, and Eva could feel that they were getting very excited. Eva was wondering what Fred had to offer and went down on her knees to open his trousers and see his tool.

She was pleased. It was obviously a nice size, not too big for her newly made part, but still strong and obviously in need of some use. She helped him to get really hard with her mouth. He took her and pressed her into the bed; she opened her legs and let him take possession of her. It was very intense and beautiful, she could feel his body movement playing with her new clitorises, and she found new feelings inside her new tool that she didn't know it existed before. Eva tried to be quiet after all, on such a small boat you can hear your neighbors very well. There were some unexpected waves coming to the boat that night, or from the boat, as it were. Yes the first try was quite a success, after they finished she could still feel him inside her, such a nice sensation, she was on the right way to get full pleasure, not there yet, well there was some learning to do on her own body.

The next morning both Fred and Eva were somehow late for breakfast.

"Morning, guys," said Fred.

"Probably not as good as yours, Fred," said Olympia, taking a sip of coffee.

"Did I do something wrong?" asked Fred.

At that time Eva walked up to the cockpit.

"Well, you guys can be a bit quieter in bed. We like to sleep too," said David.

Eva blushed.

"Well, Olympia, just wait until you fall in love, and we'll see who is quiet then," Linda said before bursting into laughter.

That day they were going to make a shorter trip to an island called Bequia, then on to Admiralty Bay. It was just about eighteen nautical miles, so about three hours' sailing. The weather was again fantastic, a regular breeze from the northeast, ideal sailing conditions all around.

David and Fred lifted the anchor, started the journey under motor, and then they set the sails and it was time to relax and enjoy the ride. Fred came next to Eva, and they resumed their kissing and cuddling session.

At the same time David started to talk to Olympia.

"Where do you live, Olympia?"

"I live near Basel, in Reinach. And you?"

"I live near Zurich in Dietikon, do you know it?"

"Oh, you are one of those horrible Zurich guys?" said Olympia.

"And are you one of those horrible Basel girls?" said David and they both laughed. "Your name is not very Swiss. Why?"

"Well my mother is Greek. I think that is why I have this love for sailing."

"OK, are you married?"

Olympia playfully slapped his knee. "Someone wastes no time! But oh God, no. Never been, and you?"

"I divorced two years ago but don't have any children. We were only married for three years."

"So you really like the outdoors, the sun, and the sea?"

"You bet," David said. "It's my third sailing trip; otherwise I sail in the Zurich lake. I have a small thirty-foot boat. You have to come and sail with me there."

"I would love to."

This would come to be only the beginning of the communication between Olympia and David. Later on this small trip between islands, some dolphins came up next to the boat. They were so gorgeous and fast. Everybody came to see, and at that time Fred kissed Eva quite intensely. Linda kissed Frank, and not one to ignore a trend, David started to kiss Olympia as well. Well, *Isabelle* was turning out to be a love boat after all.

They arrived in Admiralty Bay. Like most Caribbean bays, there was no real port; all the boats anchored where they could, so the first thing to do was to go slowly between the boats until they could find their ideal spot—somewhere that was close enough to the land and somehow far away from other boats, especially away from commercial boats.

Again they prepared the dinghy, though they all went to the island this time. They walked through the touristy places, and there are many of them, and then they decided to have some kind of a drink and all went for piña coladas in a bar near the beach.

"Wow, this is definitely a lovely place," said Linda.

"Yes but already with a lot of tourists. It's incredible how many tourists have been coming to the Caribbean in the last few years," said Fred. "Ten years ago there were not many here. Now they come from all over the place, Europe, the Americas, you name it. You will see some fantastic places later on that are so full. In the meantime, if I have a choice I go to less touristy places."

"That would be good, where we can have some privacy," said Eva while kissing her gorgeous lover.

"Come on, Eva, are you implying something?" said Olympia.

"No way! Just a remark," said Eva.

"We know you, girl. Love you," replied Olympia, before giving David a peck on the cheek.

For the rest of the day until dinner, the couples were by themselves. Dinner came, and they went to a local restaurant for another lovely Caribbean meal.

That evening Olympia was sleeping in David's cabin. Everyone had a ball; I don't think they even heard each other, or if they did, they were probably making it some kind of competition.

The next morning they all met for breakfast. They were all looking at each other with smirking faces, so Linda broke the ice. "So, the crew all slept well." There was a general laugh, as they all knew what they had done the night before.

The rest of the sailing trip was just as good as the beginning. They visited gorgeous places like Canouan; Mayreau with the unforgettable but very crowded Tobago Keys; Union Island; and Carriacou.

They anchored in the afternoon in Tobago Keys, a gorgeous but very busy place full of not only sailing boats but also very big motor yachts, some with helipads. Within one hour of anchoring, there were the local fishmen coming with lobster to sell. They were live, local spiny lobster; some of them were incredible sizes like six pounds. They bought three big lobster for dinner, and then there was another boat, selling weed, which they declined.

The big discussion that night was, How do you kill a lobster? Since they were grilling the beasts, Frank and Fred cut them in half. Linda and Olympia complained that they heard the poor animals scream with the pain, but once they tasted the delicious lobster, everyone forgot about the lobster cruelty.

Then there was a decision to make: to go farther south, to a new country, or to go up and visit one of the last bastions of English aristocracy, the island of Mustique. They decided on the last option.

Mustique, Eva learned, was a really special place, an island bought by some higher-up in the English empire in the fifties who gave part of it to Princess Margret. Well, without going into details she and her husband made this place a kind of paradise for the rich and famous, like Tommy Hilfiger, Shania Twain, and Mick Jagger, just to mention a few outside of the English royal family.

The only hotel on Mustique is called the Cotton House, with very high prices, but incredible experiences as well. The most famous bar is Basil's Bar, and the crew had great piña coladas there. They are supposed to be the best of the Caribbean, or at least the priciest. It is a place where you might find some very interesting and famous people having the same drink, right next to you.

One day they were having a quiet day in the sun on the deck of the boat, when all of a sudden a very large yacht anchored not too far away from them. This big, majestic stinker was a real motor yacht, with a helipad on the back side, and the helicopter took off. A good half an hour later, it came back with the pilot and what they thought was a really old man. Later that day, the boat opened on the side. There was a dinghy, probably as big as their own boat. The old man got on this so-called smaller craft and was piloted to a restaurant. They thought, *Well, some people have a lot of money, but are they happier?*

Another day in Mustique, they set anchor near a gorgeous, eighty-foot boat: *Swan*, one of the most famous sailing yachts in the world. As they were relaxing on deck, Eva and her friends saw a man with some kind of white crew uniform coming out of the *Swan*'s cockpit, carrying a folding table and two chairs. He arranged them on the bow deck of the ship and went back down inside it. Soon after there was an absolutely beautiful woman coming out and sitting in on of the chairs. Not long after the same crew member came back with a champagne bucket, a champagne bottle, and two flutes. He put them on the table, filled the flutes, and went down again. At that moment there was a gorgeous muscled guy coming up and walking to the girl; he had some aperitif snacks with him. They sat next to each other, kissing and cuddling and watching the sun go down.

Well, we're doing more or less the same thing, thought Eva, *just not so luxuriously.*

In the Caribbean, the sunset is iconic and fantastic. One of the most incredible things is the so-called green flash. It only lasts for a fraction of a second, but you can see a green light on the horizon. Superstitious people say it brings good luck.

Sometime on the way back between Canouan and Mustique, Fred looked at Eva with a smile and dropped the question, "Are you taking the pill? I have never seen you take one."

Well, that was a compliment for Eva. She answered, "No, but don't worry. You cannot make me pregnant."

"Why not?"

Here it was, her moment. "I have to tell you something, Fred. I cannot conceive children. I am a transgender woman. I was born a boy and changed my gender. I regret a lot, but my vagina cannot make children." Yes conceiving is part of being a woman and this is not possible for transgender woman, she regreted it deeply.

"Sorry? Wow, oh my god, I would never have believed that," Fred said.

When the silence drew on, Eva said, "I hope you still love me."

Fred ran a hand through his hair. "Sure, sure, sure, it is just some kind of shock that the nicest person I have ever had sex with turns out to be a transgender woman."

"I take that as a compliment." And Eva kissed him. Fred seemed to take a good day to get over this mini heart attack. The relationship continued quite strongly on the boat, but it took that one good day for the truth to be digested.

The trip was slowly coming to an end, back to St. Vincent, then on to St. Lucia before docking finally in Le Marin in Martinique. What a memorable time they had had together.

The end is always a bit sad, packing the bags, cleaning the boat, and getting ready to go back to the airport and back home. Only Eva could not pack up Fred and take him with her. He would stay with the boat for the next sailing trip, with another crew, and probably another girl. *Oh well,* she thought as she hitched a bag over her shoulder. She had been very much aware of the dangers before she even got involved.

Back Home to Switzerland

After a short stop in Basel, Eva went back to Paris. All was more or less the same, except that she had found three suitable candidates to take over the position of GM France.

"Hi, Thomas, nice to see you here in Paris," said Eva on the morning her boss arrived in the Argenteuil office.

"Hi, Eva. I'm glad that you have done such a great job here, our sales have actually increased quite significantly. I am sad you will be leaving here, but also glad you'll be coming back to the home office in Switzerland. As a matter of fact, we will be adding France to your responsibilities."

"Really! Does that mean more money?" answered Eva with a big laugh.

"We will talk about that later," Thomas said with a grin. "You know we never left you short. So let's see the three candidates and see where we go from here."

It was a long day interviewing the three candidates; all were engineering men in their late forties. In the end both Eva and Thomas agreed to hire Jacques, a Frenchman. He looked energetic and knowledgeable about the trade.

So came the end of Eva's stay in France. It had been a great six months in that magnificent country. The day had come, and Jacques was starting.

Her last week in France was quite busy as she got Jacques trained in the position. On Thursday evening she came back to Basel, but this time she didn't leave a big part of her luggage behind.

On Friday evening the girls got together, again in a nice restaurant near Basel, called Schloss Bottmingen.

"Hi, sisters! How are you doing?" said Eva as they were all kissing each other and sitting down.

"Probably, not as good as you, you little slut," said Linda.

Eva feigned insult. "What do you mean? I have been such a good girl. Working hard since I came back from our holidays."

They both laughed.

"OK, I am missing something here. I was the only one that was not on the sailing trip. What happened?" asked Victoria

"Oh, well, our sister Eva was very busy with the skipper in bed, and Olympia with the other guy on the boat. They made this a love boat," said Linda.

72

"Hold on! You were with your lover, too," said Eva. "And Olympia, how is David doing?"

"He is doing well. He has been showing me around Zurich. By the way we have to organize a dinner with everybody; he is coming as well. He will spend this weekend with me in here in Basel," said Olympia.

"Oh, I can hear the wedding bells ringing," said Victoria. "I should have come with all of you. I obviously missed something, well, probably not, but I am jealous."

"Your time will come, girl. You know for us it is a bit more difficult." Eva gave her a hug.

"And you? Have you been in contact with your skipper?" asked Olympia.

"Well, we talked a lot over the phone in the beginning, then he was very busy with a new crew, so we texted and slowly it's going toward silence. I never expected that he would be my lifelong partner, but it was fun while it lasted. I consider myself free again. But I am glad that it worked out for you, Olympia. David is such a gentleman."

"Linda, I hope you didn't come up too short," said Victoria.

"No, I didn't. I think some nights we were trying to make it a challenge for who could be the loudest. Anyway it was a great holiday, the sex was not on the original menu for some of us, but that came, too. The views, the food, the sailing were all magnificent. I loved it, and will do it again any time."

"Agreed, and we were so lucky with the weather," said Eva. "We never had much bad weather, only one or two showers, lots of great wind. It was a sensational time together. But next time, Victoria, you have to come."

"Yes, I will," she said. "By the way, there is a party this week at a special place here in Basel. It is a kind of organized party in a beautiful house. Do you want to come? I can get some invitations."

"That is a great idea," said Linda. "Olympia, why don't you bring David with you? Then Victoria can meet him."

"That sounds like a plan. He is coming to Basel this weekend anyway."

"All right! Let's have some fun on Saturday night," said Eva.

Friday evening, Eva got a call.

"Hi Emil, I am phoning you to ask you if are still alive. I heard you were living in France." Said Monika, Eva's mother.

"Hi Mom, how many times do I have to tell you that my name is Eva now. You are misgendering me again."

"You will always be my son, you know that. I gave a son to the world not a daughter."

"No, I cannot accept the way you treat me. Yes I am good, I was in France working, all is good." Said Eva in a very crisp way. She was clearly very nervous.

"Me and your father are doing ok but we would like to see you some time, you do not take care of us anymore."

"Well, if you welcome me as Eva probably things will change."

"Are you blackmailing me?"

"Oh never mind, just let me know what you have been up to. I hope you are healthy is good. Well you are still my parents" Said Eva

"You have to come and see us."

"Look, as I said before, I will come and see you when you treat me like the woman I am. You have to understand that." Said Eva. Well the conversation carried on, with the news from the parents, Eva was so devastated that she didn't even told her parents that she had undergone gender reassignment surgery. Their relation had almost stopped.

Saturday night arrived quickly. They all met in a bar in Steinenvordstadt in the center of Basel. There were many big kisses and hugs. David finally met Victoria. The girls had their sexiest dresses on, and the guys looked great as well. Eva was wearing a red, V-neck dress, tight and short, and some red heels, black tights, and a short black leather jacket.

They took the tram to Klein Basel and arrived at a magnificent house. They were conducted to the door, where they said their name, got a paper bracelet and then went in, pleased to learn that someone had already paid for their entry.

They came into a big hall with some white stone stairs to the first floor and a large opening to another big room. On the right side of the entry there was a coat check, so they left their heavy coats there. They were told that the music and dancing would be in the room next door, and on the first floor there was a buffet.

They grabbed a snack from the buffet and went downstairs. There were lots of people dancing, and a live band was playing rock music. They took turns out on the dance floor; it was a lot of fun.

As Eva was dancing, a very handsome guy walked up to her. He was tall, short brown hair, white skin and blue eyes, an apparent body builder, dressing with some jeans, a black shirt, and a blue blazer and smelling a very discrete parfum. "Hi, I believe you are Eva," he said. "I saw your photo at Thomas's office, the group photo with the management. Thomas told me everything about you."

This came as a not-unpleasant surprise. "Wow! And who may I say I am talking to?" she said. "I am afraid Thomas left me in the dark."

"Oh! I am so sorry, my name is Uri. I'm from Basel, a local guy."

"Nice to meet you, Uri."

His blue eyes raked over her body. "You look even better than in the picture. You look astonishing."

"Thank you," said Eva. "You look very nice yourself—well, I have never seen a picture of you, but you sure have the advantage." Looking at him, she started to feel kind of fragile, as though she wasn't sure what he would do if he knew her secret. She covered it up with a laugh.

"So who invited to this party?" he asked.

"One of my friends has the right connections. And you?"

"I am a friend of the organizer."

Out of nowhere Eva noticed three heads peeking around the buffet to eavesdrop on her conversation.

"Oh, let me introduce you to my friends." They were all looking to see what was going on—incredibly nosy.

"So this is Victoria," she said. "Then we have Olympia and David and Linda and Frank. And this is Uri. He saw my picture at the office; he knows Thomas and knows all about me."

"Oh, wow," said the girls, and they proceeded to greet him.

"Would you like to dance with me, Eva?" asked Uri very gallantly.

"Sure, if you insist."

They started to dance, and oh, he was a good-looking man, and quite a good dancer as well. They danced for quite a while. He only had eyes for her, and somehow she for him.

Suddenly he said, "I am getting thirsty. Let's grab something to drink."

Eva followed him, and they walked to the first floor.

Uri asked for a glass of water while he was waiting for his cocktail to be made. "Thomas didn't tell me that you were such a good dancer," he said. "He probably didn't tell me everything."

Eva gave a short laugh and asked, "So how did you meet Thomas?"

"We were together at the technical university, and we have been friends for many years. I am not working as an engineer anymore. Now I am in finance, but we are both in Switzerland."

"Nice! Well, as you know, I work for Thomas as a key account manager, international sales specialist, and sometimes even general manager of sister companies. But it is fun and we have a great team. I like it."

"Yes, that is what Thomas told me. I am not sure how long we will be together tonight since you are with your friends, so how can I contact you tomorrow? I want to catch up with you."

They exchanged cards, got their drinks, and went back down to the group where they carried on dancing. It was an incredible evening. Victoria had found a guy that danced with her the whole time as well, and they were all having fun. They left in the wee hours of the morning, pouring themselves into taxis to get home safely.

Sunday was a lazy morning for everyone, and Eva got up quite late. She did her usual Sunday routine, taking care of her body, using a good hair shampoo and mask, a face mask, epilation, whatever she had to do to look good. She than had a nice brunch, looked at her social media and the news.

As she was scrolling through an article, she got a text from Victoria. "Hi, sister, anything for today?"

She answered, "Hi Victoria. Barely up and alive, nothing special today. Why don't you come by? We have not had a real girls' day for ages, miss you a lot."

"You always know what I am up to, incredible, love you. See you in a while, bringing the wine."

It did not take long for the doorbell to ring, and Victoria was on the other side.

"Hi, sister, nice to see you again," Eva greeted her with a smile.

"Same here! You have been away for too long—in France for over six months, doing your sailing... We have not had time for each other for. I miss you a lot, you know that? I mean, you are my family!"

"Aw, give me a hug. I have been having a great time, I know it's not always easy but it was still a great time. But unfortunately some things were just left out. I know you were one of them, and I am so sorry."

"Don't be sorry, let's just catch up. I am sure we have a lot to talk about."

"Yes, girl," Eva cheered. "Let's sit down; I will get some snacks. It will be great with this wonderful cabernet you brought." They finally sat down and started to talk.

"I know that I have been living in stealth mode for a while now," said Eva, "not seeing any of our transgender brothers and sisters, but people have to understand that I have been very busy. Surgery, then getting better, being sent to Paris, it has taken a lot of my time and resources. But I am sure I will come to next month's meeting. It will be really great to see some of the sisters; I am sure they will have a thousand questions."

"You bet! Last meeting everybody was asking what happened with you, if you were OK. They were all missing you," said Victoria.

"I know. I got so many texts and emails saying, 'How are you? When will we see you again?' Believe me I was moved. I was actually thinking of organizing a dinner with our more intimate friends, you know who I mean." She lightly touched Victoria's shoulder. "And you, tell me what is going on with you?"

"Well, on the job side, I have been quite happy and OK, like you I have been lucky and am still on the job. But I am glad that I do not travel as much as you do. I have been doing quite a lot of local projects. Nobody has any clue that I am trans, and everything is going well." She sighed and blew her hair out of her face. "My love life is more difficult. Sometimes I see some chasers, but you know, it's always a short thing. Yes, I do have pleasure, but it's not long-lasting and so sometimes it's frustrating. Yesterday it was funny, I was dancing with a guy that I had slept with before. We had a nice time some months ago, he was OK but not interested in relationships. Probably he'll change his mind."

"Oh, that is nice, and do you think he is going to call you?"

"Oh no, for him sex is just a kink. Anyway he is bi, not what I am personally looking for."

Eva raised an eyebrow. "And what are you looking for?"

"I am looking for my knight in shining armor to ride in on a beautiful, white horse that takes me and makes me his queen. You know the old romance. And I do not mind if the knight is a boy or a girl. You know girls are better for me," said Victoria.

"Me too, but let's face it. At our age most of the knights are already taken, or we take the divorced ones. That is OK, but for a transgender girl, it's just a bit more difficult. How are you going to justify that you are a girl with something extra between your legs? And what am I going to tell the knight? That I was born a boy?"

"I know what you mean," Victoria said. "The chasers just want sex but no relationship. Most of them are married anyway. They always go back to their wife and kids, and I am getting very fed up. And then they get jealous if I have another man? It's just ridiculous. I cannot live with complete cowards that tell me to my face, 'I cannot live without you, you are the love of my life,' and then go home with no communication for four days, then if they see me on the street with another man text me saying, 'How dare you go out with another man, am I not good enough?' The story of my life."

"I hear you, sister," said Eva. "I prefer to be without sex or only have sex on my terms. When we were in the boat, I had a great time. He was a real gentleman, but I knew from the start that it wouldn't be anything. Skippers are not faithful, and he already forgot me. But at least I had great compliments. He asked me if I was taking the pill, he didn't want to make me pregnant."

Victoria's jaw dropped. "No... Oh my god, that is the nicest question! I have to have my pussy done by the same doctor."

They both laughed.

"Next time I have to go around with my pussy surgery certificate that says that I am a female but not able to reproduce," Eva joked.

"Yes, take a photo on your phone that you can show them."

"Good idea. But you know these guys always make promises, but most don't keep them. Yesterday that guy I was dancing with wanted my phone number. Well, nothing has happened so far; we will see."

"Sometimes I think I would be better off with a woman. I mean gay men will not touch us, that is clear, so either straight men or lesbian women. I do prefer men, but I feel more at ease with women. And after all it's the heart not the part that plays a role. Probably another transgender person would be OK," said Victoria.

"I agree. It has been a long time I was with a woman, well, loving a woman, and now it would not be the same thing, but I have heard of lesbian post-op sisters."

Both girls were really talking when Eva's phone beeped.

"Sorry, sister," Eva said. "What is going on here, on a Sunday?" She looked at the phone. "Oh my god! Uri just texted me, wow."

Victoria leaned closer to see "Speak of the devil."

The text said, "Hi Sexy, are you recovering from last night? Loved to dance with you."

Eva answered, "Wow, Gorgeous, already up... Yes me too, loved to dance with you."

"So when are we going to have a quiet dinner together?" Uri wanted to know. "I still have to know everything that Thomas never told me."

"Ok, ready to see you anytime, I will be around this week, just not Monday and Tuesday."

"Got it, you are booked for Wednesday dinner, will let you know where and when."

"SLAP (Sounds Like A Plan)"

"Oh, I like your humor, love."

"mmmm cannot wait"

At that last text, both girls started laughing.

"Well, the wind is on again. I better start setting the sails," said Eva.

"You see?" Victoria said. "There is hope. I hope mine texts me as well."

"Yes, you are right, hope is great," Eva said, "but sometimes it's together with fear: How will he accept me when he knows I am trans? Well, at least I have the right parts between my legs, but what will his reaction be when he sees my childhood pictures? And if things go further, when he finds out I cannot be a baby factory."

"Yes, sister, that is somehow our truth, and we cannot do anything about it. You know cis women have issues as well, but not as difficult as ours."

"Yes, you are so right, but we learn from our difficulties, and it makes us stronger, when we survive," said Eva.

Victoria looked solemn. "I see so many girls committing suicide and doing completely stupid, destructive things to their beautiful selves. Sometimes it makes me very sad."

Eva did her best to lift Victoria's spirits, and both women enjoyed a wonderful evening. They cooked, ate, and drank together.

"This was really a great day to be with you today," said Victoria as she put on her coat to leave. "I can really talk to you, we have such similar lives and attitudes. I have one thing I want to talk about before I go, and only my big sister can help."

Eva noticed a tear in her friend's eye. "Oh you are getting emotional. This must be important."

"Yes, very. I am thinking really hard about having the final surgery."

"Oh, give me a hug! Of course I will be here for you. Do you have any questions? Any worries or fears?"

"Well, it has always been my dream, but I am so scared. It is a big, big change, you know. And then the right doctor, being alone... I have so many questions, I don't even know where to start."

Eva persuaded Victoria to hang her coat back up and led her back to the couch. "You can only start from the beginning, there is no other way. Did you already talk to your psychiatrist?"

"No, but he asked me, because of the papers. You know I can only change my birth certificate when I have a pussy certificate."

"I know, the question is does he think you are far enough along in therapy ,to do this? This is not a small change and you cannot put your penis back on."

"He thinks I am ready. I think he knows more about me than myself sometimes."

"I hope so, he is a professional!" said Eva with a laugh. "At least I think so. Well, let's talk about this, there are many factors to think about. I will start with the first question: Do you want to be penetrated by a man? Between the legs, I mean?"

Victoria quirked an eyebrow. "Of course, what kind of question is that?"

Eva shook her head. "I mean it very seriously. You have to give up something that you have been using for ages."

"Oh, I know, but I hate it anyway. It's a source of pain, I have to tuck it all the time, it's not fun you know."

"Of course I do. That will be the first question your surgeon will ask, but you have to give the answer to yourself as well. The next topic will be the letters from your psychiatrists. And the third is who will be the surgeon. There are many ways of doing it and you have to find the one is most appropriate for you. I would start to have some appointments with the best doctors. If they are far away, they usually make Skype calls. I will be with you at least for the first one, if not for all.

"I propose of course the doctor that did it to me. He is in Thailand. I will send you the details. But then I would also try to see a local doctor, probably the one at the University Hospital in Zurich, then the usual ones in the US. Oh don't forget to ask your health insurance if they pay or not, you have to tell that to the doctors. I had to pay for my surgery in Thailand."

"OK let me get a little more organized and then I'll get back to you," said Victoria. "I will keep you posted about the meetings. I would love for you to come with me, you are my real sister. The other ones will go crazy when I tell them anyway. And I will tell you as well when the next club meeting is."

"Perfect!" Eva couldn't help breaking into a big smile. "I am so happy for you. You will see, it's not going to be easy, but it will be great."

The next week Eva had intense days at the office, getting in touch with her customers, including some she had somehow put behind. She was planning sales, planning and organizing customer visits, talking with industry peers to find out what was going on internationally. She managed to get her schedule organized again and her trips. There were exhibitions, various international trips and trade shows, and support trip to France to visit Jacques.

Wednesday's dinner with Uri was confirmed. They were going to a very nice restaurant in the center of Basel, the Atlantis, a fun place with a dance floor and a disco vibe, as well as a fantastic patio, which was especially nice on warm days.

Eva came home from work a bit early on Wednesday night. She got ready, wearing black leather trousers, a coral chiffon blouse with a decent but sexy neckline, a black leather jacket, and some stiletto shoes. She topped it all off with a set of gold earrings, a bracelet, and a necklace. She drove her black coupe C-class Mercedes to the Elizabethan Parkhouse and walked to the Atlantis with incredible punctuality—well, five minutes late, to make sure she was not the first to arrive. She entered the restaurant, and was asked if she had a reservation. Almost immediately Hans-Juerg, the owner of the Atlantis, saw her and walked toward her.

"Hi Eva," he said, "I have not seen you for ages. You look amazing, wow, wow, wow!" He gave her the usual three kisses.

"Hi Hans-Juerg, me too. I missed you like hell. How are your parties going? I have been abroad now for a while."

"Yes, I heard you were in France for a while, you have to tell me everything. Anyway, Uri is waiting for you upstairs on the patio, I will walk with you there."

Eva couldn't help smiling. Basel, small town, everybody knows everything even before it happens.

"Oh," she said. "You know Uri as well?"

"Oh, baby, you know I know everybody in this town." Hans-Juerg laughed. "He is a great guy. Anyway, you guys will get along just fine."

"What do you mean by that?" asked Eva, laughing in reply as they took the lift to the upstairs deck.

"I can see you both together just wonderfully."

"So, what do I have to know about Uri?"

"Oh, you will know him very well soon enough. He likes to travel, have nice parties, dance, you guys just fit like a glove. Just be square with him, he is a good person," said Hans-Juerg as they arrived at the table where Uri was waiting.

Yes, thought Eva *I will certainly be square with him, I will tell him all the details about me, but when the time comes, not from the beginning. I mean I am quite passable if it is only a one day thing, I will not tell, if it is a real relation I will have to expose myself. It is scary, how will he react?*

"Hi, Eva, so nice to see you again," said Uri as he got up to kiss her. " I see you already met Hans-Juerg."

"Eva and I have been friends for a long time,for a time she was a real real regular here." said Hans-Juerg.

"Well, we are in Basel," said Eva by way of explanation as she kissed Uri. Hans-Juerg took the chair to help Eva sit down.

"So, I will leave you love birds, I have to work. See you soon." Off he went to greet his next guests; his disappearance was soon followed by the appearance of a waiter who brought the menus.

Eva could finally put her full attention on her date. "Hi, Uri," she said with a smile. "It is very nice to be with you, and in this place. I have spent so many evenings here, Saturdays until four a.m., dancing like there was no tomorrow—well, that was a long time ago."

"Well! And I thought that I knew all about you, but the disco queen, I didn't," said Uri.

"Well, what *did* Thomas tell you about me?" asked Eva.

"He told me that you were a great saleswoman, a very good manager, that you know a lot of languages, countries, and people. He certainly thinks a lot about you. The question I have is what else do I have to know that he didn't tell me?"

The waiter came by and they placed their orders: steak tartare, spicy hot, for Eva, and a truffle burger for Uri. They agreed to split a bottle of fantastic Italian wine.

"Where were we?" Uri asked as the waiter left the table. "Oh, you were going to tell me about yourself."

"Well, I am a hard-working girl, I travel a lot, I like sailing, diving, fast cars, good food and drink, beautiful places, nature... I suppose I'm just a normal person, and you?"

"I can already see that we have things in common. I like to travel, I like nice cars, haven't sailed much but sometimes, I like shooting, alpine sports, and good living."

"I just came from holidays in the Caribbean," said Eva. "We saw some great places in the Grenadines. Have you been there?"

Uri pulled a face. "Not really. I work in finance management, and the Caribbean is kind of an issue because there is so much money laundering there. In Switzerland there is a special ethics commission for people that work for finance; it is led by the police and you have to report any money laundering or mafia money you come across. If you don't do it properly you can lose your license. I am sure it would not be an issue to go to the Caribbean on holidays, but you might have some people knocking on your door asking questions. I mean, even not far away. If you go quite often to Amsterdam, you can be sure you will one day have a police officer knocking on your door, asking you if you know about the dangers of pot. That is Switzerland," said Uri.

"That is incredible," Eva said. "I know because I know someone that used to go to Russia for business and he had the same issue. One day he had two policemen telling him about the dangers of going to Russia; they were very well informed where he had been. Even asked him if he had been contacted by the police in Russia."

"Yes, in the finance world, there are always some abuses, and our trade makes sure that there is adequate control to make sure that we are protected. The worst are the Americans, you know that many Swiss banks don't even allow accounts from American citizens or people that live in the US because of money laundering issues and tax evasion. Remember, one of the richest men in

Switzerland is an American that cannot even go back to the US. If he does, he'll go to prison on tax evasion. For many years there were many Swiss banks that were using the bank secrecy laws to support tax evasion and other special issues; the result is that they had and are still paying incredibly large fines, some in the billions of dollars range. The IRS in the US is the worst. So, like I said, I try not to do things that can be seen as dangerous."

"Well, I think that is very wise," said Eva. "Why take such uncontrolled risks?"

"Yes, but regardless, yes, I do love to travel too. Lately I was in southern Italy in the area around Naples. It is great weather and the food and the quality of life are simply incredible. The Italians certainly know how to eat." As he finished, their food and wine arrived.

"Chin chin!" said Eva, holding up her glass of red wine.

"Chin chin," said Uri. He looked directly into Eva's eyes as they shared a sip.

"And what kind of car do you have?" Uri asked as he cut into his truffle burger.

"I have Mercedes Class C Coupe. It's a nice, fast car, though I will probably change it later for a fully electric car. Most of my car trips are in town; if I go far, I usually take a Plane, so this would suit my lifestyle quite well. And you what do you drive?"

"Oh, I have more than one car. Usually I drive a Range Rover, but I have a BMW Cabrio as well, a little older car, but very nice to take out on hot days. Next time I will take you out in it on Lake Zurich."

"Oh, that would be nice. And Uri, what countries have you visited?"

"Quite a lot but most of them in Europe—Spain, France, Germany, Luxemburg, the UK, well, most European countries. Sometimes I travel to see some of my customers and I only have European customers; they all tax their money in the country they live, so I always have to demand proof to make sure I will not have any issues. Not so easy these days. And you, Eva, what countries do you usually travel to?"

"Well, the list is quite incredible. I have been to about eighty countries, literally all of the European countries, many in the Americas, meaning from Canada to Argentina, with some exceptions in Latin America such as Panama, Uruguay, and smaller countries. In the Caribbean I have been to many, but not all. In Africa, I've only been to South Africa, some North African countries such as Morocco, Tunisia, Egypt, and the Seychelles. Then Israel and the UAE in the Middle East. Russia, India, China, Japan, Thailand, the

Philippines, Indonesia, Singapore, and Taiwan." She blew out a breath and locked eyes with Uri, who looked impressed. "That is about all," she summed up, "though I may have forgotten one or two."

Uri was silent for a moment. "Wow, that is impressive! And is that for business or pleasure?"

"Most of them were for business, but some were for pleasure. I mean, it is part of life."

"It must be fascinating to have been in so many place, seen so many cultures."

"Yes, I think it is very interesting, but sometimes when you travel for business you don't really have time to visit the nice places."

"Yes, that is true. I used to go to London a lot and always to the City, well the financial district, and about the fifth time I was there I realized that I had never seen Buckingham Palace. Then I decided to stay three extra days, and it was fantastic. I went to Harrod's, and King's Road, the Tate Modern, Piccadilly Circus, all the tourists traps, but at least I could say I was there."

Both had a great dinner. Uri was very gallant and paid for Eva's dinner. Afterward they walked to the Parkhouse and went their separate ways, with the promise they would be together again on Friday for dinner. Typical Swiss man no kiss on the first date.

Friday came, and Eva and Uri decided to have an aperitif just after work. They met in a bar at the Steinenvorstadt.

"Hi, Uri, how was your week?" said Eva as he greeted her with a kiss on both cheeks.

"The usual, some nice things happening in the stock market, so I am taking advantage. And you?"

"Well, I am trying to get things organized around the home office again. Things were a mess after I came back from France. I think I will start traveling again very soon."

"I would love to come with you on one of the trips—if that's not being too forward," Uri said.

"Sure, but you know it's for work. I cannot take you to the customers."

"Just wishful thinking. But you know I can join you at the end of a trip; then we come back home together."

"That would be a great idea." Eva was touched by his level of interest in her.

Uri changed the subject, perhaps so as not to show his interest too keenly. "So, do you know this one: What did one boat say to the other boat? 'Are you interested in a little *row-mance*?'"

Eva chuckled. "You're funny. OK, how do you shoot a blue elephant? With a blue elephant gun, of course."

Uri finished his aperitif and set it on the bar table. "So today it's a fun day. What would you like to do? We could go to the cinema and then have a snack, or we could have dinner."

"You know I had a long week," Eva said. "I'm not feeling up for a big date night. Let's go to eat in the Kunsthalle and we can talk."

They had a great evening again in this nice restaurant, and then they went home.

The next day they texted.

"I really liked last night," Uri's text read. "You are a very interesting person."

Eva smiled as she read this. "Thank you, you too. You have a lot of knowledge and savoir faire."

"What are your plans for the day?"

"I am going to the gym soon, then I have not yet decided. And you?"

"I have a dinner with some friends, we will probably go to the Atlantis."

"Oh, with your girlfriend?" Since he was being so slow, she wanted to have some kind of feedback, was he dating someone? Why was he taking his time?

"No, with some friends from school. We are very good friends and have the regular dinners to keep up and have fun."

"I know what you mean," she texted back. "I have the same situation with my best friends. They were with me when we met, remember?"

"Sure I do, and are you guys seeing each other this weekend?"

"Not sure, we have not planed anything, but I need some rest, too, it has been a very intense time for me at work."

"Let's go to Mulhouse on Sunday morning," he suggested. "They have a fresh market. We can get some nice things and have lunch there. I will pick you up."

"That sounds great. And let's have a nice walk together, something else other than eating, you know."

"Hahaha, agreed," texted Uri

On Sunday morning Uri picked Eva up, and they drove to the beautiful town of Mulhouse in France, on the Swiss border, and had a great day in the market, walking around and of course eating. There was a fantastic counter with cheese.

"What do you call a really good-looking piece of Swiss cheese?" Uri asked her.

Eva looked him straight in the eyes. "I don't know, what?"

"A *hole* snack."

They both laughed, and Uri took advantage of the moment to give Eva a kiss. She liked it a lot. When they pulled apart, Uri took her hand to walk down the lanes of the marketplace. They leaned in close as they inspected a flower stall, and Eva's heart started to beat faster.

"I really like you, young lady."

"I like you, too," she said. "You are funny and sweet." They had a nice, romantic late lunch, then went back home. At customs they had to declare the goods they'd bought and pay some money for the wine, but all went well.

Back in Reinach, Uri parked his car near Eva's house. They got out, opened the boot, and Uri took out Eva's purchases.

"I will help you get these inside," he said.

"Just put them there," said Eva. "I will put them away later."

Uri put her bags on the floor, looked at her, and like a slow magnet they started to kiss. The kiss grew more intense, and Eva closed the door with her leg. They started kissing more breathlessly, and soon he was taking his clothes off and she was doing the same thing. It didn't took more than five minutes before they were both naked in bed, kissing and touching each other all over.

All of a sudden Uri rolled on top of her, Eva opened her legs, and he penetrated her. Eva marveled at how naturally and fluidly this had happened, as though she didn't even have to think about it. It was somehow tight but just fantastic. Thank god she had dilated in the morning and all was still quite well lubed. They lazed about for much of the afternoon, kissing each other all over and having sex as the mood took them.

Much later the same day, they were in each other arms, waking up from a short nap.

Eva asked, "Are you thirsty, my gorgeous bull?"

"Yes, my love, I am. Wow, that was amazing. Love you, girl."

Eva left and came back with a bottle of champagne, two flutes, and some snacks. Uri opened the bottle and served them.

"Oh my god, you are amazing. I never had a lover like you," said Uri, kissing Eva on the neck before toasting her with his glass.

"Thank you, you were amazing." Eva took a sip of champagne and cleared her throat. "Uri, there is something I have to tell you, but let's do it later."

"Oh, just let's cuddle with each other."

Well, Eva wasn't one to push a subject. After all, they had gone too far, and they were happy.

They started to see each other more or less on a daily basis. Later that week, Uri was at Eva's house, and the honeymoon spirit was still very strong. Eva decided to take the plunge.

"Uri, my love, as I said on Sunday, I have to tell you something. I believe a relationship has to be based on the truth."

Uri furrowed his brow. "What is it, my love? You already said last time that you had something to tell me. Do you have some kind of sickness? Are you married to someone else? What is it?"

"OK, here it goes." She took a deep breath. "I am a transgender woman."

Uri processed this for a moment. Then he propped his head on his hand and looked at her. "Well, you are a woman, OK, so what? You are telling me that you were a man before?"

Eva's heart was beating quickly again. "Yes, my love."

"Oh, that is a new one for me." Uri licked his lips in thought, then shrugged. "But you are a woman now. Come on, let's go to bed. I want to possess you again, all the way."

Uri was a real bull; he certainly liked his sex and they were doing it very nicely. Somehow, though, after this news the relationship went on for a bit but their connection started to fade away.

Uri was very respectful but eventually admitted that he did have some issues with Eva's news after all. Though he certainly enjoyed the sex and always came back for it, Eva had noticed a change in him.

Traveling Around Again

Eva didn't have long to be sad about Uri. She was back in business and needed to see her clients worldwide; there was a lot to catch up on.

It was a Saturday in April. Spring was coming up, and it was beautiful outside. She had not seen Uri for a couple of weeks. He kept telling her he was busy; he probably had another girlfriend. Eva put her luggage in the car and drove to the Zurich airport. There was not much traffic, so she was there in under an hour.

Eva went through the check-in area and through duty free and was in the glamorous shopping and restaurant area, waiting for her flight to São Paulo, Brazil. She then went to the second floor and to the Swiss Lounge. She was admitted, took the elevator to the top floor, got a glass of champagne and some nuts, and sat down. She then checked her email and texts in the phone.

There was one from Uri: "Have a nice flight, can't wait to be with you again." And on the group text, all the girls said, "Enjoy Brazil."

Before long, Eva had gone through customs and immigration, been bumped up to business class, and boarded her plane.

"Hi," said the man in the seat next to her.

"Hi," Eva answered.

"So, another long flight. Going on business or pleasure?"

"Business as usual, and you?"

"Same as you," said her neighbor. He was a young man with a short beard and was quite nice-looking. Eva was almost sure he was gay. They did not speak much but were very nice to each other.

Finally, the plane took off. As usual, Eva was busy taking photos from her window seat. She was really fascinated by airborne photography. Flying out of Zurich gave her some fantastic views of the Alps on the way to Africa, before making the Atlantic crossing to Recife and finally going down to São Paulo.

The flight attendant came through and at Eva's request topped off her champagne. The food in business class was quite good; she had a choice and she took the lobster ravioli with a great sauce, and some wine. She slept very nicely for a good four or five hours, then she was thinking about her life, Uri, the girls, and everything that had been happening to her lately, ever since she returned from Thailand.

Eva landed very early in São Paulo, about six a.m. She took a taxi and went to her hotel in the expensive center of the city. Well she always booked the same hotels, either the Address Faria

Lima or The Unique. Since the company was paying, she had opted for the Address. She had an early reservation, so she could take a shower and rest. At about one in the afternoon, Claudio, the representative for Brazil would come and get her for lunch. She prepared herself, with nice, professional makeup, a short, blue print dress, beige heel, and her usual black bag.

A couple of minutes before one, she came down to the lobby to wait for Claudio. She had waited less than five minutes when Claudio and his wife arrived.

"Oi, Claudio, how are you? Oi, Luisa, and you?" Eva said, greeting them in a customary Portuguese fashion.

"Oi, Eva, great pleasure to see you here. You look great as usual," said Claudio. This was accompanied by kisses all over the place, Brazilian style.

"Marcilio and his wife will join us for lunch. They are really looking forward to see you. So today there will be not much business, more of a private 'getting to know you'; tomorrow you can give them the presentation," said Claudio as they began walking to the car.

Luisa was looking at Eva with a kind of jealous look, and Eva couldn't really blame her. She had a very good-looking, Brazilian husband, and Eva knew that he was not exactly the most faithful, like all Brazilians, and he was going to travel with Eva for the next days. She was not sure if he was not going to try something with her, but she tried not to worry. From all of her dealings with him, Eva knew that Claudio was a real gentleman.

"Luisa," Eva said, "how are the kids? And your family?"

With this tactful change of the subject, Luisa brightened. "Oh, Eva, it is nice to see you here again. The kids are doing great; they are with their grandmother today, I really needed a day out; having kids is really a full-time job. How was your trip? You must be exhausted. You arrived very early this morning."

"I am all right, I had some time to rest and get ready, and the weather is so nice here. In Switzerland it is now getting hotter but still far from nice weather."

"We heard that you were in France for a long time. What happened?" said Claudio.

"I will tell you everything at lunch. Where are we going?"

"There is a great Argentinian restaurant in the shopping center of Cidade Jardim. Marcilio will meet us there; it is on the top floor, very nice view and real great food."

They drove to Cidade Jardim, which was only about ten minutes away, parked, and took the lift to the top floor. The elevator door opened up to pure, blue sky. Eva found herself surrounded by open-air restaurants and, right in front of her, a shop called Tools & Toys. It seemed to sell helicopters and boats, the real thing, not miniatures. Eva filed it away as a good place to meet people.

"Oi Marcilio, *tudo bem*?" said Eva. She saw him standing with his wife, Tina, in front of a really luxurious Sikorsky helicopter.

"All good, Eva. Come, let's sit down inside of this little helicopter. It's an incredible machine, and it costs twelve million US dollars," said Marcilio. They entered the luxurious helicopter. It was quite incredible with a bar, black leather seats, and all the accoutrements.

"Wow, so when are you going to buy one, Marcilio?"

He laughed. "Oh, I am afraid the company I work for is not paying enough. But it is nice to see how the top 1 % lives."

"I have the same issue, my company does not pay enough, well you know that Eva" said Claudio. "I am hungry, let's go for lunch, troops."

They started to walk to the Argentinian restaurant, and Eva looked at Tina. "Hi, girl! We even didn't say hello. How are you doing? You have to tell me everything about your wedding." Tina and Marcilio had only recently gotten married. It was Tina's first wedding, and Marcilio's third.

They arrived at the restaurant, and the waiter walked them to the table where they sat down.

"Tina, Marcilio, I have something for you, a late wedding present." Eva opened her bag and took out a very beautiful, decorated box, and gave it to Tina.

Tina opened the box to reveal two wooden elephant statues decorated with silver plating.

"Oh my god, how nice! They are really gorgeous," said Tina.

"Elephants in many civilizations are signs for strength, luck, and happiness, and this is what I wish for you," said Eva. "Tell me about your wedding, how was it?"

"Well, you can imagine, for us it was the most fantastic day of our lives. We had about three hundred guests, and we were expecting you," said Tina. "The weather was great, and we did everything outdoors. Since it was at night we had a lot of torches to illuminate the way; we did in a very nice garden, similar to a miniature botanic garden. I loved it."

"Yes, I saw the photos and was very impressed, you know I was not able to come to Brazil at that time, I was sent to France. " said Eva.

"Thank you. The ceremony was done by a friend of ours that is priest; my father got me down the aisle and we finally said yes." As she said that she looked with a very lovely smile at her husband. "For the rest of the evening, we had a great buffet with all the Brazilian specialties: *feijoada*, grilled *picanha*, fish dishes, it was very good. Afterward there was a big party; we left at about midnight, but the party went on till something like four a.m."

"Wow, I am so glad for you! It sounds like you had a lot of fun."

"What about you, Eva? We heard that you were in France for a long time," said Claudio.

"Yes, I was helping Thomas there. The French GM left, and there was some cleaning up to do, but it was a great time."

"And about your love life? When are you going to get married?" asked Tina playfully.

"I have a boyfriend, but I don't think I will marry him," Eva deflected the question. "Right now we don't have too much time for each other. We are both very busy."

It was a great Sunday. They had a very good lunch, a nice beef barbecue dish from Argentina, chimichurri, an even better wine—a malbec from Mendoza—and great conversation. That night Eva went to bed early, as she was quite tired, and the next day, she had the start of a working week.

On Monday Claudio picked her up from the hotel. They had the first customer visit in the morning in São Paulo; then they drove to an airport in nearby Congonhas to fly to Curitiba in the south of Brazil. This airport is in the middle of São Paulo, and it is very scary to say that you literally look into the living rooms of people when the planes take off or land.

Arriving in Curitiba, Claudio rented a car, and they drove to Jaraguá do Sul, the town where the customer was. That night they had dinner with the customer, a very nice evening.

For the whole week they traveled between the south of Brazil and São Paulo, visiting different customers. It was a good time to promote the company, and Eva managed to get some orders as well.

Thursday arrived, and she was back in São Paulo. That night she was going to her preferred place, a bar called Charles Edwards that had live music, an incredible selection of whiskey, and many reserved bottles with the names of the owners plastered across them. There were lots of nice people there, male and female.

In the beginning Eva went with Claudio, and they had dinner together.

"I will take you back to the hotel now," said Claudio, checking his watch. "I have to go. My wife gets very jealous if I stay long."

"No, I would like to stay a bit longer. Don't worry, I know my way around and I will take a taxi to the hotel. The music is so fantastic. I can't leave just yet," said Eva.

"Are you sure? You know São Paulo is dangerous."

"I will be all right, Claudio, and thank you very much for the great support here."

"OK then, if you're sure. Bye-bye, enjoy, and don't be foolish."

Claudio went back home to his wife and Eva was alone there, meaning not so alone. It didn't take long for a nice, muscled guy to walk up to her and ask her to dance. The music was very loud, and they danced for a long time. Sometimes there was slow music, and they started to dance very close to each other. Eva could smell him and feel his beard in her face. Wow, she was getting turned on. He kept trying to touch her lower back. Then he kissed her on the neck.

"What is your name, my love?" he asked.

"Eva, and you, gorgeous?"

"My name is Ari."

"Oh you are a smooth mover, boy," said Eva. He gave her a very beautiful smile. Wow, she was getting hot.

"Can I get you something to drink, Eva?"

"OK." He went to the bar and she followed. He got two full champagne glasses and toasted with her.

"Come with me," he said and she followed him to a quieter place in the bar where they could talk.

"You sexy girl, what are you doing here all alone?" Ari asked.

"Having fun, and you?"

He just smiled back and said, "Me too," and kissed her in the mouth. She was so hot, and waiting for it. They stayed glued together for some time.

"Where are you from?" he asked. "You have an accent, although I can see you speak Portuguese very well."

"I am Swiss, I am going back home tomorrow," she said.

"Do you come here often?"

"Yes, many times in the year."

"Do you have a car or can I take you to the hotel?"

She raised an eyebrow. "Oh, you are in a hurry," she said

"I am." He kissed her again in the lips. "What about you?"

They went to the entrance of the bar together, cuddling all the way. He gave a ticket to the valet and quite fast his car was parked in front of the bar. It was a nice, big Mercedes, quite unusual for Brazil. They both entered the car, and Ari asked,

"Where is your hotel?"

She leaned into him, showing him the hotel name and address. For this, she got another kiss, and soon they were driving to the hotel.

"When is your flight?" asked Ari.

"In the evening, but I do not have to work tomorrow."

"OK, and what are you doing here?"

"I am working, visiting customers for my products. I have many customers in Brazil; it's a great place for business."

"And you like Brazilian men?"

"Why do you ask?"

"Because tonight I will make you crazy with joy, my love."

Soon they were at the hotel, and he came up to her room with her. When they got to the room, Ari embraced her and kissed her passionately; then he started to undress her and kissed her all over. Eva started to take his shirt out of his pants, kissing and nipping at every inch of exposed skin on his incredible, muscular body. They finished undressing and lay in bed next to each other, naked. They kissed all over and had an incredible night of intense sex, obviously safe sex, Eva always had some condoms available, and it was a good way of getting lube without too many explinations.

The next day she texted Claudio that she was somewhat indisposed and was going directly to the airport. Ari left around lunchtime; they promised to text each other and stay in touch. He wanted to invite her to his house the next time she was in town.

The time came in the afternoon, and she took a taxi from the hotel to the airport, and flew back to Switzerland.

Arriving very early Saturday in Zurich, she got her car and drove home, where she went directly to bed. As she arrived, she texted Uri "Back home, honey, how have you been?"

She did not get an answer straight away, so she figured he was still sleeping. At this point Eva's expectation on this relationship was not very alive anymore, things had changed.

She woke up just after noon, took a shower, and got her stuff organized, washed, and got everything organized in her closet, ready for the next trip. She started to text with her friends, Linda, Olympia, and Victoria; they organized a small brunch for the next day. Uri still hadn't answered. She was getting a bit worried and tried to call him. He didn't answer that either.

The next day she met her friends at the Moevenpick in the marketplace in Basel for the brunch.

They greeted each other with kisses and hugs. The boyfriends were there as well, Eva reluctantly noted, so it was more than just the four of them.

Where is Uri?" asked Linda.

"I don't know," Eva said. "I texted him yesterday, he didn't answer, and then I phoned and nobody answered. I am a bit worried. If I don't hear from him until this evening I will go to his house and see if he is OK."

"You probably should not. You know he is still fighting with the idea of having a trans girlfriend, give him some space," said Victoria. "To be honest, and I hate to say this, I am not sure if this will have a future."

"Anyway," Linda said, trying to change the subject, "how was your Brazil trip, girl?"

"The usual, it was pleasant but the usual routine."

"Everybody, I have something to say," said Frank. He waited to make sure they were all listening to him. "I popped the question!" Linda showed them all her finger and the magnificent engagement ring, a solitaire diamond of at least two carats set in a gold setting.

"Oh my god," said Olympia, a sentiment that was echoed by everybody present.

"Are we going to have a wedding? When? Have you already decided?" said Eva.

"Within the next two months, and you three are going to be my bridesmaids, so I need your help. We have to find a wedding dress, dresses for you, and I need some advice to get the party working. I have to count on you girls," said Linda and everybody hugged each other.

At that moment Eva's telephone made a short sound with the notification that a message had just come in. She was somewhat disturbed and reached out for the phone to look at the message, which was from Uri: "Let's get together later today, say at 5pm at Molino, just for a drink."

Well, that didn't sound right, but she answered, "Sure, love, see you later."

"What is going on, Eva?" asked Victoria.

"Uri just asked me for a drink later today. I wonder. Anyway, Linda, you have to put up a schedule for all the activities. I want to be with you girls, and you know I travel a lot."

"Can we get together next Thursday after work to look for the wedding dress?" Linda said. "I will tell you exactly where. I want something nice and I think it is going to be very short notice. I mean, two or three months for a good dress could be short."

"Done it's already on the agenda," said all the girls.

"We are going to have a civil wedding. We are not part of any church, and then we will have a small ceremony in Schloss Binningen with a kind of guru and have dinner there. We don't know how many people yet, and we are looking at possible dates, but I was thinking an evening wedding would be great."

"Yes, evening weddings are very nice," said Eva. "In Brazil I just saw Marcilio and his wife; they just got married as well, and it was also an evening wedding."

The girls started to put the plans together and talked for a long time about the colors of the bridesmaids' dresses, what to eat, and so on. The guys, who had also become good friends, busied themselves talking about business.

The day passed and five p.m. arrived faster than Eva had planned. She went to the Molino restaurant, already with a good sense of what was going to happen. She saw Uri at a table near the bar and joined him.

"Hi, Uri," she said.

He seemed resigned, if polite. "Hi, Eva, how was your trip? Was it OK?"

"Yes, I had a lovely trip. How have you been?"

"I've been all right. Well, I think you already know what I want to tell you, but I cannot live with the idea that you were a man. I'm so sorry, but I cannot tell that to my family and friends."

Somehow it hurt less than Eva had thought it would. "OK, so we're breaking up, right?"

"Right, I am more of a society person than I even thought. I like you very much and want to tell you that I admire your courage and how beautiful you are. We had a great time together, but it's over."

"OK, and when did you decide that?"

He scratched his head sheepishly. "You know, some months ago, but now I have someone else I like, so we have to say goodbye. Yes, I did enjoy the sex and my time with you, but I am too conservative to go any further. I want to get married one day and have kids with my wife, and you cannot give me that."

"OK, I understand," she said. "Let's move on. I need time to digest all of this."

Eva stood up and walked to the car. Her heart was broken, but the news was not really a surprise. She had expected it; she noticed how his behavior had changed after she shared her truth with him. It had been clear for some time that he just came for the sex, but now he had found someone, a more proper someone in his eyes, and it was over. She texted her friends, and they were very understanding and all gave her their love.

Monday came, and Eva planned two trips, one to India and the other to China. There was an international exhibition she had to attend in Shanghai, and she had to visit some very important clients in India later in the year.

Thursday came, and it was time for late-night shopping. Eva met up with Linda and the others at this fantastic bridal place called White Secret Bridal. They all sat down after the usual kisses and hugs, and Linda disappeared into the back of the shop to try on some things.

"So, now you are finished with Uri?" said Victoria.

"Yes, sister, the next page in the story of my life is coming, another day, another guy." Eva tried her best to laugh it off.

"Yes, but why?"

"He loved the sex, he loved me somewhat, but he could not come to terms that I was transgender, even if I had sex reassignment surgery and all. He wants a woman who can give him a child and that he does not have to tell his parents and friends was born a male. You know how it is, the church obliges, and they follow, or whatever. It is a real danger for us. It really takes a courageous and great man to accept us as we are."

"I am so sorry," said Olympia. "Trans women really seem to have a challenge with relationships."

"I know, you know for me it is even worse. Most men that are looking for us are already married, and they are just looking for sex," said Victoria.

"You know I believe that if the right knight comes along, then he will be OK. But it's definitely a special person," said Eva. She didn't want to think about Uri anymore, and so she was pleased to see Linda walking back into the dressing room. "Look, look! The first dress is coming."

Linda entered the room wearing a fantastic, white mermaid dress. It was lace on a silk base with spaghetti straps, a very tight fit and quite a long train. It was exquisite and fitted her beautifully shaped feminine body. Linda was more a southern type woman with shoulder length black hair, dark brown eyes and a very slightly tanned complexion. She was always very well groomed, painted nails in strong colors, always with a very nice but not intense make up.

"Oh my god, you just look amazing," said Olympia.

"Mm, actually, this fits you so nice, but I would add probably a short lace jacket or a gorgeous tulle veil," said Eva.

"I do agree with Eva and Olympia, gorgeous; it fits you so well," said Victoria.

"Come and help me girls." Linda walked up and down, looking at herself in the mirror. "On a scale from one to five, five being the best, what would you give it?"

It was anonymous; all gave a ten. The dress was really pretty.

"Mmm, you are not being critical enough. But I do like it. Let me try another one." And she left the room with the fitter.

"Wow, that was something! Really nice. I am so jealous, I wish I could look so good in such a dress," said Victoria.

Both the other girls backed up and said, "You are not the only one, sister!"

It didn't take long before Linda came out in a second outfit. This time it was a white satin ballgown with a kind of corset, quite nice, but not exactly her style.

"OK, I thought the last one was better for you. Somehow you now look like a meringue. You have such a beautiful, slim figure, and this dress does not bring that into light," said Eva.

"I think you are right," said Linda. She scanned her audience. "Points?"

All the girls gave between one and two points, agreeing that it was not really for her. She went back and forth, trying on. A total of about ten dresses, and the one that got the most points was the first one. Linda put the first dress on again and came back.

"Well, girl, I think we all agree. This fits you like a beauty, it was made for you," said Olympia. Eva and Victoria could not agree more.

"Thank you, girls, I think you are right. The first was the best." Linda put on her best American accident to say, "I say yes to the dress."

They all laughed, Linda got dressed, and it was a girls' night out at the bar. With the news of Uri being out of the picture, Eva filled them in on all the details of her encounter with Ari in Brazil.

Saturday night Victoria and Eva went out together. They went for dinner at the Atlantis, quite late to enjoy the dancing.

"Hi sister, nice to see you again," said Victoria. "So no traveling?"

"Oh, give me a break," Eva moaned. "I just came back one week ago from Brazil, and now I have two trips lined up, one for China and the other for India. I just want to make sure that I am around for Linda's wedding and of course when we go to try on our bridesmaids' dresses. I am so happy for her."

"Me too, I am so happy for Linda—and for Olympia. David seems to be quite a nice guy."

"Yes, he is. He was such a gentleman during the sailing holiday, and they seem to stick together. My big question is whether Olympia is going to Zurich or if David is coming to Basel. That is a tough one."

"Yes, you are right. Hmm. They should get a place halfway between the two cities. Like that all would be good for their friends to visit," said Victoria. She sighed and swirled her drink. "I wish I had a David, you know?"

"But we have so many more issues to find partners," Eva said. "It's just like we were talking about on Thursday. Sometimes I regret being trans. All the men want you for sex but no commitments; it's kind of tough."

As though the universe or God or whomever had heard, Eva noticed that the table next to them was full of women, and all of a sudden one of them started to talk to Eva and Victoria.

"Hi, girls, I would like to give you a glass of champagne. My name is Yvonne, you seem to be so alone."

"Thank you, Yvonne, we certainly accept," said Eva, and they received the glasses "Cheers, everyone, you guys are great. My name is Eva, and this is my best friend, Victoria."

"Hi, everybody," said Victoria.

Yvonne's friends introduced themselves as Brigitte, Lisa, and Ana.

"And what is the occasion?" asked Eva, holding her champagne flute aloft.

"Well, it's Yvonne's birthday," said Ana.

"Oh, let us sing 'Happy Birthday'!" Eva saw Hans-Juerg and asked him, "Do you have a cake? It's my new friend Yvonne's birthday, you know. Can I give that to the girls?"

Hans-Juerg came close to her and whispered in Eva's ear. "Sure I can, I will get a cake for all the girls, but Eva, you know they are in a lesbian club, right?"

"Oh, interesting information," said Eva.

The cake came some minutes later, and both tables kind of merged into one. They were all talking a lot, and being very nice to each other.

"Now we have a cake, Yvonne, again, happy birthday, girl," Eva said. Yvonne blew out a single candle.

"We didn't know how old you are, so they just put one candle, to make it less of an issue. See? No discrimination," said Victoria.

"You girls are great," said Yvonne. "Come and join us, we don't bite—well, not yet."

It was clear by now that the other women were lesbian. Some even started to kiss each other, but that was not really an issue with Victoria and Eva.

Eva exchanged telephone numbers with Yvonne, and Victoria with a lot of girls in the group. They had a great night, finishing up on the dance floor. It got very late, and Eva had too much to drink, so she took a taxi home, telling herself that the next day she would get her car from the garage. As it turned out, she was not the only with this idea.

The next afternoon, she took a taxi to the garage. She had no makeup on and was not particularly well dressed. She left the taxi and entered the garage, only to find herself face to face with Yvonne.

"Wow, what a small world! What are you doing here?" said Yvonne.

"Probably the same as you, getting my car," said Eva and gave her a kiss in greeting.

"What a coincidence. Let's get the cars and meet for a coffee, but not in the center. Where do want to go?"

"Your call, love."

"Let's meet at La Columbiana in the Güterstrasse in Gundeli."

"OK, done."

They both got their cars and drove to the coffee shop. It was not so easy to find a parking place, but they met there.

They ordered their coffees, and sat down at a table to wait for them.

"So one year older, how do you feel?" said Eva.

"OK, I don't see the big difference," said Yvonne. "I'm still me, and I am having fun with a stunning girl."

Eva grinned. "Really? Tell me everything about her."

"Well she has long, brown hair, brown eyes, and is sitting next to me. You know her?"

"OK, I am not so stunning. Meanwhile you are beautiful. Just look at you! You are very slender, with your gorgeous, green eyes and blonde hair, wow," Eva said.

"Not as cute as you. I sure would like to touch your breasts. What size implants did you put in, girl?"

"Oh, you have been X-raying me?"

Yvonne winked, looking a bit like a sexy version of the Big Bad Wolf. "You bet."

"What else did you see?"

"A lot, but the rest I will tell you somewhere else."

"Did you see that I am a transgender woman?" said Eva. Eva had decided after her heartache with Uri not to waste any time telling possible romantic partners her truth. She had especially heard of TERFs, some cruel lesbians who only accepted cis women as women, and she wanted to make sure Yvonne was not part of this.

"What, no way! Not an issue for me, but you have to tell me something. What will I find between your legs?"

"Same as you, a vagina."

Oh, I am relieved. I think we should carry on with the coffee in my house, you know."

Eva pulled back a little. "But I hardly know you, I am confused."

"Oh, come on, you are just as attracted to me as I am to you. Let's just find out about each other."

Eva couldn't argue with that. They went to Yvonne's house. As they opened the door, they started to kiss each other, undressing each other piece by piece, and walking to the bedroom. Then they lay down. Yvonne trailed kisses down Eva's stomach and they proceeded to eat each other out, followed by kisses and some intense orgasms. Eva was getting so aroused by the way Yvonne touched her all over the body, sometimes in places she didn't even know she had any feelings. The tenderness and at same time firmness Yvonne touched her around her new vagina, was like an immediate orgasm. After some rest and some champagne, they repeated the scene. It was a long and fantastic affair.

It was well into the morning when Eva went home. She had just enough time to get dressed and go to the office.

She arrived at the office at the same time as Thomas. "Morning, Thomas, how are you doing?" said Eva.

"I'm well. So, did you had a nice weekend?" he asked.

Eva bit her tongue, not sure how much she wanted to tell her boss. "I have such a lot to do. I'll catch up with you later." And she went to her office.

Thomas's eyes were wide, and he followed her inside.

"Is everything OK?" he asked. "You sound and look kind of exhausted."

"Yes, I had a great weekend, too great. And you?" asked Eva.

"I had a very quiet one with the family. Well, I will have to see you a bit later. We had some enquiries from Dubai, and I was wondering if you didn't want to go there on the way to Bangalore."

"OK." Eva forced a smile. "Let's talk later."

Even as Thomas headed out of the office, Eva was thinking to herself, 'Did I hear this right? He wants me to go to Dubai? One of the most transphobic places in the world? What shall I do?

Tell him no? I have to talk to my best friend about this.'

It didn't take long for her to whip out her phone and text Victoria and the girls. "Alarm!" she wrote. "The boss wants me to go and visit a customer in Dubai, not sure what to do, this is a very dangerous zone for transgender people."

Her telephone went hot with answers.

Victoria wrote "Tell NO this is such a transphobic country, that is if they let you in."

Linda wrote "Only do this if you are comfortable, it's your life that is at risk."

Olympia, "I agree with the girls, but legally your papers say you are a woman and you have a vagina, so they will not even notice you trans."

Eva answered "Thanks for your words, I think I will take a chance. Have to talk with Thomas."

And then she wrote again, "Oh, and you will never believe this, but this time I have a girlfriend."

Again the telephone went red hot with messages.

One was from Victoria: "I am meeting Lisa tonight, she already had the message from your incredible night with Yvonne, you slut. LOL"

Olympia said "You visiting Lesbos girl, wow Love it, love is love anyway. Enjoy."

Later that day Eva went to Thomas's office and said, "OK, I will go to Dubai, but can you increase my insurance please?"

Thomas frowned. "What do you mean?"

"Well, Dubai is not really a nice place for girls like me, but I will just go and see the client and come out again. Anyway, my papers are all correct, I have all the right parts, so I don't think they will suspect that I am transgender."

"Oh, I see. Well, don't worry, I will have someone to escort you, you have nothing to worry."

The rest of the week was quiet, meaning Yvonne and Eva were in bed every day, and were together all the time. They really started to get to know each other, and had a great time.

The last time that Eva was with a girl like that, she was still living as a man. Yes sex was very different, she had a penis and she was than the active part but it was not exactly fantastic, a lot of stress and hard work to have an orgasm. Sex with a man was for her very fulfilling, mainly since she had her surgery, she always preferred to be possessed, it was kind of more normal for her. Lesbian sex was something completely different because there is more the sense of sharing the feelings with your partner and please each other, some men only please themselves during sex.

That weekend the girls were all on their own, meaning Linda and Olympia were with Frank and David respectively, Eva was with Yvonne, and yes, Victoria and Lisa were getting to know each other.

The next Thursday, the girls came together at a very chic boutique in Basel; they were going to try on bridesmaid dresses that Linda had chosen. They were identical, and thank God Linda had great taste because they fit everybody just fine.

New Feelings

On a Saturday some weeks later, everybody went out for dinner. On Sunday Eva was going to leave for Dubai and then India. Among the four couples, there were six girls and two lonely guys, but well, that is life.

There were the usual kisses and hugs, and then they sat at their table in a really nice restaurant.

"Everyone," said Eva, "let me present you to my girlfriend, Yvonne. We met some weeks ago and have been getting to know each other since then."

"And I want to present my girlfriend, Lisa," said Victoria. "We have been together for a few weeks as well."

"I am sorry to ask, but I am kind of very surprised to see you with a woman, Eva," said Linda. "I always saw you with men, what happened?"

"Wow, that is a direct question," said Eva. "I thought I was straight, but now I know I am either bisexual or pansexual, meaning that I am attracted to any gender. I have my definition, but it's about hearts not parts. And I am very much in love with Yvonne."

"Oh, that is nice," said Linda.

"We love you the way you are," said Frank.

They had a wonderful dinner, discussing their friendships, and love lives.

"OK, everybody," said Frank. "We have a date for our wedding. It's going to be on June 23, a Friday, so please reserve it in your diaries."

That night Yvonne slept in Eva's house in Reinach.

Eva was cooking. She made a vegetarian Indian dish of curried lentils, basmati rice, and spinach with cheese curds, served with white wine. They were very relaxed and started to kiss and cuddle. It was a very nice and sensual evening.

On Sunday, Eva got up early, got ready, and finished packing her bags. She went to the side of the bed where Yvonne was still sleeping and gave her a big, deep kiss. She couldn't believe how quickly she'd fallen in love with this woman.

"I have to go, baby," said Eva.

Yvonne woke and gave Eva a groggy smile. "Yes, you do that, tiger. Please stay safe and text me and phone me all the time. I want to hear from you. It's going to be a long trip, and I want to know what happens to you. Please be very careful in Dubai."

They kissed again; it was very hard to be away from each other.

Eva drove to the airport and boarded the plane. This time she had no upgrade, but it was OK. She had a good place in economy.

She arrived at dinnertime in Dubai. She was scared when she went through customs, but she gave her Swiss passport where "Female" was clearly written as her gender, so they let her in. There was a driver waiting for her at the airport who drove her directly to the hotel. She texted Yvonne as soon as she got to the airport: "All good, flight was OK, going through customs, soon." After the customs: "I was really scared but all went well, I am through the customs, going to the taxi, will phone you as soon as I am in the hotel."

Eva had a room in a hotel near the Dubai marina not too far from one of the palm islands, but near the main road that goes everywhere in the city.

It was a very luxurious, beautiful hotel, and very expensive.

Eva called Yvonne using WhatsApp. "Hi, girl, how are you doing? I just arrived to the hotel. What a place!"

"Hi, mi love, I already miss you, and you are gone for another week. I don't know how I am going to survive."

"Of course you will survive. Don't worry."

"So tell me about your trip."

"No issues, the food was horrible, airplane economy class horrible, but I am here and all good. I am going to have dinner at the restaurant of the hotel, not going out, it's so incredible hot. You cannot live here without air conditioning around here."

"Yes, I can imagine"

"The lights of the city when we were landing were just amazing. It's an incredible, completely artificial city. And the cars here? My Mercedes looks like a maid's car. There are so many Rolls Royces, Ferraris, Maybachs, Lamborghinis, just incredible. Next time you have to come, though I'm not sure we can survive as lesbians here."

The next day Eva was picked up early by her chauffeur. She had a great visit with the Arabic customer, a local factory. Most of the workers were from India, but they liked good quality and had good money to pay it. The customer took her to lunch near the center of Dubai, in the jewelry souk. Eva checked out some of the jewelry stores there, and she was overly impressed. The first thin that was unusual was to see the women wearing a black burka, where the only things you can see are the eyes, the hands, the very expensive handbags, and when they walk you can see the shoes. Some of the women's hands were decorated with henna. All the Arabic women have this burka. The Europeans in Dubai dressed more or less as usual, but with no miniskirts or even shorts, everybody has to cover the knees. The Arabic men have a white Jalabiya and their red-and-white head cover with the black ring.

The Jewelry Souk in Dubai is the most incredible market in the world. All jewelry is sold by the kilo, and the kilo of gold there is not very high. From the most kitsch gold and diamond pieces to Rolex watches with black diamonds, to much simpler pieces, Eva could find all there. Rings, earrings, necklaces, belts, jewelry, shoes, some things were beyond belief, like in the Scheherazade or *The 1,001 Nights*. Eva bought some modest pieces for herself and Yvonne.

After lunch they had a meeting with some engineers, and the customer drove her to the Dubai Mall. It was one of the most luxurious malls in the world, with an artificial lake built in the desert, and of course the Burj Khalifa, the tallest building in the world. Eva went up to the 140th floor, the highest point on the 163-story building accessible to tourists. The extra twenty-three floors didn't matter. Eva was already so high up that there were clouds between her position and the ground, and with the light show on the pond below, this was an astonishing view.

"My love, you should be here with me," she told Yvonne over the phone. "This place is of such an incredible, totally artificial beauty, it is almost unbelievable to understand that about forty years ago this place didn't exist. It was a desert, and now it's just simply a place of extreme richness. They say, 'In Dubai you buy,' well I already did and everything here is tax free and the prices are unbelievable. Not staying long tomorrow, I leave for Bangalore in India."

"My love, you take care, I really miss you. What did you buy?"

"I bought you something in gold from the souk. You will see when I get back, and I hope you like it. But you cannot believe it: at the entry of the mall there is a poster that tells you everything that is forbidden. Alcohol and smoke I can understand, but no miniskirts or shorts, and it's forbidden to show signs of affection."

"What do you mean by that?" asked Yvonne.

"You cannot kiss or cuddle in the mall; otherwise you can land in prison. Well, the list of don'ts is quite extensive, believe me. I could not live here. And for transgender people it's unbelievable. I know a famous transgender person from the US that was not allowed in. But I must say the Dubai Mall is mostly the same stuff we get in the west, just considerably cheaper. Oh, something interesting, most people here are from other countries, not many locals, but they are really rich."

The next morning, Eva took a plane to Bangalore. She was happy to leave such a dangerous zone behind her, especially without having had any problems, though she hadn't done anything that could be considered dangerous and had kept quiet.

As Eva refocused her attention on her upcoming customer meeting, she recalled the profound and astonishing images she'd been left with on her last trip to India. Sure, there were images of poverty, but also of the country's incredible richness and culture that is very different from the west. Eva always found this country fascinating; she loved it and had seen its incredible evolution over the years, including the rise of the middle class, something that barely existed in India some decades ago.

As far as transgender people are concerned, Eva wasn't worried. India was a nation that had had transgender gods and where transgender people have coexisted with cis people for many centuries. During the British colonization they were outlawed, but later, some years after India became independent, they reintegrated the transgender community. This community is huge in India and still a harbinger of good luck for Hindus.

Sunjeev, the MD of Thunder in India, was waiting for Eva at the airport, but her time in Bangalore was cut short. They flew the same day to New Delhi where they stayed the night at a hotel near the airport.

"So, Eva, tomorrow we are going to have a long car trip to the Haridwar, but you know the place already, you know how it is," said Sunjeev at baggage claim.

"Oh yes, we know the way, or at least your chauffeur does. You know there are only a handful of countries that I refuse to drive in, and India is one of them."

"Yes, I can understand. The traffic is very diverse and challenging here. When was the last time you came to India? I cannot recall."

"I came last year, but I do remember the old Bangalore airport. That was a real disaster, and the new one is so nice."

"You are so right, but you know the old one was a military airfield that was transformed into a public airport. It was in the wrong place and much too small. Bangalore had a tremendous growth, and the old airport could not keep up."

Eva called Yvonne that night from the hotel room in New Delhi. "So, my love, pray for me. Tomorrow I will go from New Delhi to Haridwar, a town in the south of the Himalayas, I think one of the first towns that the Ganges River encounters in the north Indian valley. It is a Hindu sacred town, so no alcohol and no meat, and once a year they have a big festival with millions of people, and many of them bathe in the river to purify themselves, well over one million of them. The issue is that to get there we have to go probably one hundred and twenty miles, but it takes something like five hours. That road is incredible, it is mostly a dirt road with two lanes, driving English style—for us on the wrong side of the road—but everybody uses this road: cars, trucks, bicycles, motorbikes, horses and carts, people on foot, holy cows and buffalos, people on horseback, and they all have different speeds. Then you have to think of the carts with the hay that are so overloaded they barely can move. Some of the bikes are transporting goods, God knows how they manage, and then there are the cars that are in a hurry, all of that in the same road. It's unbelievable, every time I arrive on the other side of a journey in India I think it's a miracle. Can you imagine, if one of the drivers of these Indian tripods has a tire blowout, he just changes it in the middle of the road. And be careful, this road is completely full of cars."

"Wow, you go to some wild places," Yvonne said with a chuckle. "Send me some pictures. In my heart I am with you all the time. I love you, Eva."

The next day Eva, Sunjeev, and their driver headed to Haridwar, on the usual road with the usual challenges, but it was still a great experience. The next day after the customer visit, they went to see the temple on the banks of the Ganges. The temple had different statues honoring Brahma, Vishnu, and, of course, Shiva. Shiva has a very strong meaning for transgender people because the god presents both as female and male. Eva always had this incredible feeling when she was near temples, and this was no exception.

They went back to New Delhi and flew to the wonderful city of Bhopal, where Eva had to give a speech to a circle of engineers visiting from different Thunder customers. Eva always stayed at one incredible hotel in Bhopal, the Jehan Numa Palace Hotel, and that was where the meeting was scheduled to take place. Staying in the hotel was like going back to colonial times, and it was the only hotel she knew that had a horse track through its gardens. Top hotels in India are some of the most incredible ones in the world; the service is just amazing. Eva remembered one of the times she was staying in this hotel, and they had a three-day wedding ceremony with over two thousand guests in the gardens. Indian splendor remained, in Eva's opinion, the most incredible in the world.

Eva's presentation went well, and she caught up with Sanjeev the next morning.

"Hi, Sunjeev, let's go for breakfast," she said.

"Hi, Eva, great speech. Did you sleep well?"

"Oh yes, I was talking well into the night with my friend."

"Oh, you have a friend? And what's his name?"

"My girlfriend is called Yvonne. She is from Basel, a nice person."

"Oh, OK. It was really a nice show yesterday; all the engineers were very impressed by your presentation."

"Thank you, I enjoyed it as well; it is always great to talk to your brilliant people. Das was explaining to me about how difficult it is to get into an Indian university. I was impressed; he told me that for one place in an engineering university there are literally thousands of applicants, so they only choose the best. He said it is easier comparatively to go to Harvard."

"Yes, that is correct. It is not easy to get in at all. India has some of the most incredible minds."

"Yes, I have learned that, and I have to say some of the greatest cooks and styles of cuisine as well. I am dying for some dal. I love it, but it is a bit spicy for breakfast."

After Bhopal, Eva went to another holy city, Vadodara, but this time they could buy some wine at the government shop, only she got a stamp in her passport saying that, well, she was an alcoholic. After a short stay in Mumbai, they went back to Bangalore. Eva was staying at the LaLiT Ashok, another great Indian hotel.

One evening, she had some Brazilian customers coming to eat with her at the hotel. They had opened a factory in India, and they had sent a technical team there to inspect the site. Now, Eva knew that Brazilian and Indian people come from two very different cultures that do not necessarily get along well. The Brazilians are meat lovers and do not eat necessarily very spicy food, most Indians do not eat meat and everything is spicy, so the marriage is somewhat difficult. The nights at the Lalit, though, featured a more European and South American style of food and drink, so her Brazilian customers loved it, beef, shrimp, all the good things and not necessarily hot.

The time came, finally, to go back to Switzerland. Eva had another long flight from Bangalore to Zurich, with a short stop in Frankfurt.

She went home on a Friday afternoon. That evening Yvonne came back to her, and they had a great night together. Eva showed Yvonne the photos and the films she took on her phone, and they caught up on some much-needed cuddles and kisses.

The relationship between Yvonne and Eva was really taking off, but with it there was an air of jealousy and suspicion brewing.

"Are you telling me everything, my love?" said Yvonne after Eva had cycled through all of her camera roll from India.

"Sure, my heart, I am telling you everything."

"You are not forgetting the affair you had with some nice, muscular guy? I mean, you like men a lot. Are you sure that I am enough for you?"

Eva put her phone away. She had to wonder if her Brazilian customers had brought the subject to the top of Yvonne's mind. "You are always asking the same question, Yvonne. You have to learn to trust me. I am not cheating on you."

These conversations had been kind of soft in the beginning, but with time and with Eva's various travels, they had started to get heavier and heavier. Slowly the trust was going away.

Linda's wedding date was coming in a hurry, and Eva still didn't have a gift for her. They'd been friends for so long that Eva felt a lot of pressure for it to be a nice one. Eva and Yvonne soured all the shops to find something good; finally they found a set of Lalique decorative glasses with a beautiful woman's figure. They cost a fortune, but were very impressive.

Some days before the wedding, all the bridesmaids, the groom, and the best man had a meeting about what was going to happen during the ceremony. Eva was thrilled when she, Victoria, Olympia, and Linda had the opportunity to have a dinner together, just the four of them.

"So, Linda, you must be absolutely nervous. The most beautiful day in your life is coming soon!" said Eva.

"I am so nervous. The idea that I am compromising the rest of my life with someone, well, yes, I am ready for it, but it is still an incredible idea. Then there is all the nervousness of putting up a show for two hundred people; it's a lot at the same time." She took a deep breath and seemed more centered when she blew it out. "So, yes, I am looking forward to it. Anyway, girls, thank you for your support and friendship."

"Of course," said Olympia. "So, we have organized the bachelorette party for you. We will pick you up on the Thursday before the wedding at seven o'clock. The rest is secret, love."

"And be prepared for a late night with a lot of alcohol, since Friday you will not go to work anyway," said Victoria.

"You girls are unbelievable, but please nothing that is too much. On Friday evening I have to look like a princess, don't forget."

"Don't worry, we will take good care of you. Nice fun and games," said Victoria.

"By the way, Victoria, how are you doing with your Lisa?" Linda asked.

"I love her so much and she loves me too. We are having a great time getting to know each other. Last week we did a small trip to Alsace, had great food, and bought a lot of wine. We had to pay at customs, but we got Riesling and TOK, so good. And Olympia, how are things going for you and David?"

"Oh, things are nice and hot," Olympia said with a waggle of her eyebrows. "We are thinking of moving together, probably in the fall. The issue is that we don't know where yet: in Zurich or Basel, or even somewhere in the middle. But we probably will stay in the Zurich area. Anyway it has a great train to come to Basel, so I won't be far away. No more than Eva with all of her business trips."

"Speaking of, what about you, Eva? How are you doing?" said Linda.

"All good, had a good trip to India, and still alive after Dubai, but I will tell you the details next time," said Eva.

"Well, what about Yvonne, all good?" said Victoria.

"Yes, yes," Eva said.

"That didn't sound very convincing, girl. Let us know if you need any help," said Linda.

Eva thanked her for that and quickly changed the subject.

Next time they would be together was for the bachelorette party, with another twenty of Linda's friends.

The evening finally came, and all the girls were dressed in sexy, casual clothing. Some wore dresses, some just plain jeans and some kind of sexy top. They all met in the center of Kleinbasel and went to the first floor of a restaurant where they had a small room reserved for them. There was a long table and some space there. They all sat down.

"Dear Linda, we are all gathered here to bury your freedom," said Eva. "Yes, we are making a hole in the ground and putting your freedom inside with the hope that a tree of beauty, fertility, kids, and toys will grow in its place. Yes, it is a very big change to your life, and we, your friends, will be behind you."

Everyone cheered and clapped at her toast.

Olympia's speech followed Eva's. "Oh, dear, now you officially have the right and duty to share your life with Frank, your childhood sweetheart and forever love. This is such a big step, but also a beautiful and loving one, so what are you looking for? Home, kids, and all that goes with it, I can only say, Oh god I am so jealous, but my time will come too. Love you and we'll always be with you, but before the new life, we have to bury the old one. Kisses, sister."

"Well, I am the last of the four musketeers," said Victoria as she stood from the table. "Last, but not least. Throughout many years, we met regularly, we talked about our wishes, our bad times, our good times, and it has been a blessing to tell you, I love you, sister. Now you are changing your life. You will be sharing it with the love of your life, the time to procreate, to expand your family and create a different future. Well, let's celebrate what you have achieved and hope that the future only brings what you hoped for. Love you, sister."

At that time there was a strong knock at the door. Victoria opened the door to reveal a policeman. He strode into the room with a piece of paper in his hands.

"Hi, where is Linda?" he said in a loud voice.

Everybody was looking puzzled and looking at each other. Victoria said, "Linda is here at the end of the table." The policeman walked toward her, and when he was close to her, he said, "Linda, I have to arrest you!"

"Sorry, what did I do wrong?" answered Linda.

At that time the policeman grabbed his shirt and with a strong motion tore it off to reveal a gorgeous torso, and then, with a similar movement his pants came off, leaving him with just a small speedo.

The ladies cheered.

"You have been accused of murder," he shouted over the applause, "for killing your freedom." There was laughter and a general ahh of admiration for this gorgeous stripper.

He made sure Linda was sitting at the end of the table where he had some room, and he started to dance and get her to touch his body, his torso going down to his legs. The dance carried on, and he lifted everything. Some of the girls were getting quite hot and hysterical, but all in all it was a nice and positive night. Only Yvonne who was sitting next to Eva didn't seem to be having a good time. This was mainly because she gawked at Eva's obvious excitement as she stared at the guy's body.

Well, the party got very drunk, with many laughs and a lot of fun. Linda's single life was over; now she could carry on with her life, together with her Frank.

Finally, marriage was in the air. Olympia, Victoria, and Eva went to Linda's house to help her get dressed. They all looked and felt incredible. Linda's wedding dress was just fantastic, even more so than when she had tried it on. She looked elegant in her makeup and hair style, a bit sexy, but simply beautiful. Her hair had been done earlier in the day by a top hairdresser in Basel, and her makeup was done by a professional from Globus as well. Everything matched. The girls were wearing identical, long, mauve chiffon dresses with a very nice V-neck. They had also gone to the hairdresser and had their makeup done by the same Globus expert.

All went well. There were some tears at some points during the day, but they were very reserved and trying not to show their nerves.

Linda was so happy. She kept explaining that her friends just looked perfect. The photographer came and took some pictures of the bride and her bridesmaids all together. The three girls headed to Schloss Binningen together, while Linda drove with her father, who was very formally dressed.

The girls arrived a bit early, checked if everything was right, and texted Linda about everything. Some moments later, the master of ceremonies asked all the guests to sit down. Frank and the best man were already in place, and the girls went out to the car where Linda had arrived, helped her out, and helped het to get to the house, lifting her dress so that it would not get dirty. Linda's father got himself to position, and on the signal, he entered the room with the stunning bride by his side and the three bridesmaids following behind. The bride was given to the groom, and the master of ceremonies started the wedding.

It was a beautiful ceremony, and when the "I dos" had been said, there was a kiss, a big clapping of hands, and all were happy.

After the ceremony, everyone went to another room for a seated dinner, where everybody had specific seating arrangements. Olympia was sitting next to David, Victoria with Lisa, and Eva with Yvonne at the same table along with a couple of other people. After dinner, they started with all the speeches, and of course, the three girls did a shared speech with a picture slideshow of their friendship, ending with all their love and best wishes to Linda. Some of the old pictures showed Victoria and Eva when they were much younger and presented as men. That was somehow a big shock to some of the people in the room, but it just showed a wonderful friendship that went beyond the gender boundaries.

It had indeed been a beautiful and amazing ceremony. After the speeches were said and the plates were cleared, they started to dance. Eva danced most of the time with Yvonne, but all of a sudden, Hans, a transgender man, that they all knew came up to her and asked her to dance. Eva said yes, to the horror of Yvonne, who, it turns out, was really an incredibly jealous person. Eva noticed the issue with Yvonne and she stopped dancing with Hans, but it kind of got their relationship off on a bad foot again.

Linda and Frank had a great day. The food was good, the people were wonderful, and all went just as planned. After the wedding they went away for two weeks on their honeymoon; they refused to tell their friends where they were going.

About a month later all the girls got back together. They all had had their own summer holidays, and a lot to tell.

It was a beautiful day, so the girls decided to go to the Wasserturm Bruderholz and eat outside.

After the usual welcomes and kisses, they sat down and ordered something to eat.

"Linda, where did you go for your honeymoon? We cannot wait to hear everything," said Eva.

"Yes, time to drop all the secrets, sister," said Olympia.

"Your wedding was like a fairy tale," Victoria said. "I am heavily thinking of marrying as well, so let it all about your honeymoon."

"OK, fine, I will tell all my secrets," said Linda. "Well, the night of the wedding we actually slept in the rooms of the Binningen Castle. The next morning we went to the airport very early, and we flew to Mexico City with a stop in Amsterdam. We stayed three days in Mexico City. It was really great, we went to see the Chapultepec gardens, the anthropology museum of Mexico City, the Plaza de la Constitution, all the famous spots there. And we ate like royalty. We loved the place; it was a really beautiful except for the horrible traffic. Then we flew to Merida in the Yucatán. Frank found this fantastic hotel there called Hacienda Kaan near Valladolid. We spent about three days looking at the cenotes and even diving there. Those are beautiful holes with rivers and lakes on the bottom, just fantastic. We went diving and had such a great time together. Then we went to Cancun for the rest of the trip. Just a great holiday destination; we just chilled and enjoyed having some time with each other."

"That sounds marvelous," said Olympia. "And what a great destination."

"Yes, you bet! We were dancing with the mariachis and having the lovely Mexican food. We really had a treat, and guess what?" Linda leaned forward a little bit, eyes shining. "I stopped taking the pill. I want to get pregnant."

"Linda, you want to enter motherhood? That's great! So plans are there in the horizon. We are all going to be aunts," said Victoria.

"We are so glad for you, and how was the sex? Well, the honeymoon sex," asked Eva.

"We had some unforgettable moments, and not only with the sex. I certainly recommend Mexico for a great holiday. What about you? What did you girls do?"

"OK, I'll go next," said Victoria. "Lisa and I decided to have a real lesbian holiday, so we went to Miami. I has some contacts from the trans community there, and we met them in Florida. We went to a very LGBT friendly place called Wilton Manors, and we had a great time. We were invited to a great lesbian party. Oh my god, the girls had fun, with strippers and all! It was incredible; they were from all ages, old girls, very young ones, and we all had a blast.

"We were even invited to a very special, private evening. It got very sexual. I was kind of embarrassed, and Lisa was quite excited, in the end we just enjoyed it, and there were no jealousy. But it was quite incredible to look at the butch girls and the girly ones. Anyway it actually made our relationship stronger. Oh! And one thing, we saw some pictures of friends from when they had their lesbian wedding. We were so jealous. I hope Switzerland changes its laws on gay marriage soon; it's not fair. Probably we will go to Las Vegas and get wedding."

"Wow! Those were some sexual holidays, and no jealousy?" said Eva.

"None whatsoever. Lisa is so nice and accepting of everything. Anyway I do not travel as much as you, girl," said Victoria. "What did you get up to?"

"Well I broke up with Yvonne," Eva admitted. "She was getting more and more jealous. While that was happening Hans, a trans man, invited me to dance at Linda's wedding. It went kind of forgotten for a couple of days, but then Hans started to text me regularly. I tried to put him off, but he kind of continued. I must say, it's my fault as well, I should have blocked him and I didn't. Well, Yvonne found out, and she just left with a text for me to go to Hans.

"I had started to get fed up with her eternal jealousies and constant discussions about it, so in the end I was happy to see her go. In the end I ended up in bed with Hans. It was a very nice night, we had fun, but he is not really my type, he is too pushy for my liking. He thinks he has to to have an opinion on everything, I think his testosterone just got to be too much for him. Yes we had some nice days together. The sex was kind of interesting but fun, but that is over too. In the end I stayed at home for most of my holiday. I went for a couple of days to Lugano just for fun. I tell you, it's over for me with relationships." The girls started to protest, but she held up a hand. "Come on, it is always the same thing. I am not like you girls, I cannot keep a person for a long time. I just don't know what to do, so I'm over the whole shit."

"Oh, girl, you just have been unlucky," Linda said. "Anyway you should make up your mind about what you want: a man, a woman, a trans man or a trans woman. I'm not clear at all with who to set you up with."

"Well, I told you, I am pansexual. It's the hearts, not the parts."

"OK, but the parts matter as well." said Victoria, and they all laughed.

"Don't worry, girl, you will find your white knight, too, whatever their parts are," said Olympia. "You know now I have David. He has been fantastic, but I spent many years trying as well without results, and I was only dating cis men, so I didn't have the choice. And I had my bad days as well. You will grow out of it, sister. We love you."

"Yes, yes, but anyway, it's your turn, sister. Let us know what you did," said Eva.

Olympia gave Eva one more look to make sure she was OK. When Eva waved her hand, gesturing for Olympia to continue, she shrugged and turned to the group. "Well, you know David loves sailing, so we spent a week sailing to Palma de Mallorca with a skipper. We had a great time and great weather. We had two days on the island, looked around, it was packed with people, mainly the usual Germans drinking like there was no tomorrow, then we went to the Palma de Mallorca port and we met our skipper. We sailed to Ibiza, then to the Island of Formentera, then back to Isla Redonda. The remaining days we were in the south area of Palma.

"We really enjoyed it. David is such a good cook, he was doing everything for us, and we really had a great time. The only issue was finding a place in a port; twice we had to anchor outside port because it was full, and even when anchoring the boats were always too close to each other. We had a couple of very romantic nights as well, and you know we are moving in together. I will go and live near Zurich and work in Basel, at least for the time being. I mean, all my customers are in Basel. You know I have my own cabinet now and work mainly for the pharma industry. The good thing is that my office is in the center and has good access from the Basel train station. It is easier for me than for David, and he has a great house anyway. I will let you know when we move. And you, Eva, when are you traveling again?"

"Very soon, I have a tour around the world planned. First Zurich to New York, then going to Schenectady in New York State, then Chicago, Tokyo, staying for a couple of days, and then going to Hong Kong, Singapore, and Shanghai, then coming back home. It's going to be a huge trip. I am really worried; the logistics will not be easy."

A Big Trip This Time

Eva was planning her tour around the world; it would be her first such trip. If you go from east to west on such a tour, you lose one day of your life because of the time difference. If you go west to east, you actually gain one day. That is great, but if you have a customer plan, it is difficult to change.

The first day of her trip arrived. On a Saturday morning, Eva went to Zurich airport to fly to Newark, one of the New York airports, and probably the best. She had a nice trip in business class, and she tried to rest during the flight. In Newark, she rented a car and drove to New York City, where she checked into a hotel in midtown Manhattan.

New York is the most vibrant city in the world; you can stay there one year and still have many things to visit and know. For transgender people it is probably the most trans friendly place in the world. It is quite normal to see transgender girls and crossdressers all over. That night Eva had a quiet night. She went to a restaurant near Times Square, then afterward to a place to hear some live music before going to bed early. Usually if she stayed longer in the Big Apple, she would buy Broadway tickets and then see a big show, but on this trip there was not enough time for all that.

The next morning, she got up and drove to Albany, the capital of New York State. It was a three-hour trip, and her hotel in Albany was strategically positioned near Wolf Street, where a lot of restaurants and shopping places were. She didn't lose too much time to go shopping. Shopping in the US is so much cheaper than in Switzerland, and they have great stuff, so she always went shopping when she was there. She needed some clothes for the trip, and she had planned that in advance. Who could resist Victoria's Secret, Macy's, and all the other great US department stores?

On Monday she had two customers visits, and she met with the US manager of Thunder. She had good meetings and even some orders. In the evening she had a business dinner.

"So Eva, how is your company doing?" asked the customer, Willy. He was a very conservative, overweight man, a real redneck, but a nice person.

"Well, Willy, we are actually doing quite well. This year our sales have risen, and there are some new products coming to the market. I am trying to promote them worldwide, and I must say, it is going quite well. I believe we will have our best year ever. And you? How is business treating you? Medium-size companies like yours are not always easy."

"Oh, you know the big guys are taking everything. There have been so many changes in the market. First, many owners are coming to a certain age, and many do not have children to carry on the business. Others have children, but they gave them too much education and they don't want to take over the parent's company, so they sell and the big corporations are buying them all and making them even more profitable. So small shops like mine are disappearing.

"On top of that we have a government that does not prioritize business. They have reduced a lot of expenditure in the army and in infrastructure, making our life difficult."

"Oh, I see. You do not support the current president?" asked Eva.

"Of course not! He is terrible, making gay marriage legal, and all the rights for those trans people. It is a blasphemy. I am a very religious guy, and my church hates what he is doing."

"Oh, interesting," said Eva, though she thought, *Oh my god, this guy is transphobic and homophobic. I wonder what he would do with me if he knew that I am trans. Probably nothing, but you never know. And here I thought he was a nice guy.*

The evening continued. They were talking about hunting, technology, and other things, but Eva was happy that it would soon be over. There were too many rednecks in the USA, and many of her customers were rednecks anyway.

The next morning she and Willy visited some customers in the same area, and after lunch Eva drove back to Newark, returned the rental car, and flew to Cleveland. She stayed in a hotel near the airport, and she got a car. The next day she had a busy day visiting customers in Ohio. That night she had dinner with one of her distributors, during which they talked mostly business thankfully. After Cleveland she flew to Saint Louis and then to Chicago, always visiting customers. She visited some customers in the area, and on her last evening in Chicago she went for dinner at the McCormick and Schmick's near O'Hare Airport. She was sitting alone at the table, and the table next to her also had a party of one: a very good-looking man, approximately her age.

"So, alone tonight?" he asked.

"Yes, you too, apparently."

"Yes, I am on a business trip, going back home tomorrow morning," said the gentleman.

"I'm also on a business trip, but I continue my trip tomorrow. I have a long trip this time."

"Oh, nice, let me introduce myself. My name is Chris, and I am from Florida. I live in Boca Raton."

"Nice place to live. My name is Eva and I live in Switzerland, in Basel, though I'm leaving tomorrow for Asia."

"Asia is big. Where to?"

"I see you know your geography," she teased him. "Not bad, I am actually going to Tokyo."

"Wow, that is a long trip," said Chris.

"Yes, it's a pole trip, twelve hours the whole way."

"On business?"

"Yes, I have to visit some customers."

"Wow, a very international girl. So what does such a gorgeous girl do?"

"Are you talking about me?"

"Who else?"

"You're making me blush with such nice words," said Eva, who was very much enjoying the discussion.

"So? And what do you do, sexy girl?"

"I am an international salesperson for a Swiss technical firm. We sell special machines for the electrical machine industry. I do key account management and large global customers. And you, Chris? What do you do?"

"Oh, I own a company that makes technical testing equipment."

"Interesting, what kind of tests?"

"For the mechanical industry, electronic measurement equipment."

"In that case, we do very similar things. And you live in Florida?"

"Yes, Boca Raton is about one hour north of Miami."

"Nice, I have never been in Florida, but would love to come."

"Be my guest. I'm waiting for you there already," he said. "And how long have you been in international business?"

"About ten years. I always try not to travel, but because of my languages and knowledge of different cultures, I always get the international customers."

"And how many languages do you know?"

"Only six: German, French, Italian, English, Portuguese, and Spanish."

"Only six! Wow, I know only three: English, Floridian, and the love language. Well, some bad Spanish as well."

They both laughed.

"You are so funny. So what brings you to Chicago?" Eva asked.

"Same as you, visiting customers, trying to sell them something. I just had a very large contract signed with a major Canadian airplane manufacturer."

"Oh, you mean Bombardier? They are my customers but for the trains."

"Really? It's an incredible company, and still family owned. Tell me what is your background. You seem to have some knowledge, for a woman."

This, for the first time, rubbed Eva the wrong way. "What do you mean 'for a woman'? Do you think we are inferior to men?"

"No, no, no, but you know we are in America."

"What do you mean? Women are only good for kitchen, kids, and church? That is what we say in German."

"No, please do not misunderstand me. I think women are great and often much stronger than many men. After all, they try to be stronger, not all but many."

After clearing that hurdle, their conversation lasted a large part of the night. They exchanged phone numbers and email addresses and promised they would contact each other. Chris was quite intelligent and kind correct, but a man, and always trying to show it.

The next morning Eva packed, gave the car back, and went to O'Hare Airport. She checked in with United and went to the lounge for breakfast. She got a coffee, some sweets and fruit, and sat down, waiting for the time to go to the gate. She opened her computer, and started to check her emails when all of a sudden she heard,

"Good morning, pretty Eva, are you following me?"

It was Chris.

Eva turned her head, completely in shock,, and said "Oh, no, *you* are following me." She got up and they kissed each other's cheeks in greeting.

"I am going to get a coffee, please reserve that seat for me," said Chris. He left his luggage with Eva and went away. It didn't take too long before he was back and sitting next to her.

"So, gorgeous, when is your flight home?" asked Eva.

"Oh, in about one hour, I have to go to the gate in about twenty minutes. And you, pretty girl?"

"Oh, you are such a charmer. I am leaving in two hours, but have some emails to look into."

"So you are flying to Tokyo, are you business class?"

"No, but I am a very high frequent flyer so I have access to the lounges worldwide."

"Nice, I am actually flying business class, but it's only a domestic flight." He shrugged dismissively, as though not wanting to draw too much attention to his own status.

"I guess you fly a lot as well, right?"

"Yes, you know we are a medium-size company, so we have to make everything work, sales, finance, manufacturing, you name it."

They had another wonderful conversation, and again promised to stay in touch.

Some moments after Chris left, Eva got the message: "Just got inside the plane, and already miss you."

"Oh nice, you will forget me when you are at home with your wife LOL."

"I don't have a wife, yet, still looking for the perfect woman."

"Oh, good for you."

"Have a safe flight and tour of the world and say hello from me to your husband."

"I don't have a husband," answered Eva. "Still looking for Mr. Right."

Eva had a long flight to Tokyo's Narita Airport. When she arrived she had a text from Chris: "Hope you had a good flight, beautiful girl, let's stay in contact. Back to Florida, all normal and good." Well, she was liking these texts more than she expected.

Koji, the Japanese agent for Thunder, was waiting at the airport for Eva.

"Hi, Miss Eva, welcome to Japan."

"Hi, Koji, nice to see you again in your wonderful country."

"Thank you, Miss Eva. I have arranged that we use a bus to go to the hotel. You know most people do not have cars here because there is a lot of traffic and it's difficult to get a car. We usually use the subway in this city."

"Thank you, Koji." And so they took a bus to the hotel in the Ginza area, south of the center of Tokyo City. The traffic jams in this city are incredible, but they do have one of the cleanest and most organized subway systems in the world.

Eva's only issue with traveling on the subway was the names of the stations. They are usually written in Japanese, except the ones in the center, so what Eva found most convenient was to always have a map of the subway with the English translations, so you know the English name and you can compare it to the Japanese signs. It is still risky, but the only way to get around in Tokyo.

In Tokyo, everything is composed and quite beautiful; the gardens are so incredible, the restaurants, the food and the culture are just astonishingly rich. So were the prices; everything in Tokyo proper was so expensive. For the hotel rooms either one pays a fortune or has a room so small that they cannot move. Eva was staying in a western-type hotel for about hundred fifty US dollars. She got a room with one single bed, a tiny bathroom, and the size of the room was probably twice the size of the single bed. But it had something that was typically Japanese, a WC with the shower from the bottom, a great Japanese invention. It is like a mixture of WC and bidet, you use the water to clean everything afterwards, some of these WC are so sophisticated that you can control the temperature of the water and the strength of the shower, for all tastes.

Eva had a restful Sunday and did some sightseeing at the usual tourist attractions: the fish market, the Meiji Shrine, the Shinjuku national garden, the temples, and of course the very famous electronic city of Akihabara in downtown Tokyo.

During the week Eva went to see her usual customers and give some lectures. Koji was with her all the time, which was very welcome, as it is so easy to lose oneself in this city.

Food in Japan is a culture of its own; Kobe beef, for instance, is one such very special, expensive, but fantastic experience. As a matter of fact one of Eva's customers invited her for a Kobe beef dinner at an expensive restaurant where one sat tatami mats on the floor. They drank a lot, including a kind of cognac with hot water, quite strong. Typical is of course Saki, rice wine that can be drunken either hot or cold. Sushi in Japan is incredible to say the least, the choice of fish is very extensive. Most famous is Fugu, a very poisonous fish that is a big delicatessen in Japan, It is said that if the person that cut the fish wrongly and the customer died of poison he has to commit hara-kiri, a ritual suicide. Sushi is by no means the only option, and all food in this country has the most incredible presentation and is really great to eat. One of the great eating experiences Eva had was in the canteen of one of her customers. Very simply a fantastic Japanese Poke Bowl with a fantastic dark tuna.

During her stay in Japan and for the rest of the trip, Eva was exchanging texts with Chris, and it was felling more and more like love.

Eva had a very positive and rewarding stay in Japan. There were some customers that showed interest in buying some of the equipment. Doing business in Japan was quite interesting; in a meeting, there is always a boss and a lot of people around him. The boss makes all the decisions, but he does not always ask all the questions. The hierarchy of a Japanese company is very strong, and not always clear to non-Japanese people. On Japanese visit cards there is one side in English and another in Japanese; the real hierarchy level is only written in Japanese, the English is usually what they want non-Japanese people to think. The Japanese like to ask many questions, and if the decision maker does not have all the facts, the boss will carry on asking questions, either directly or through the people that are below him. It can be extremely complicated. Even so, Eva had done well.

Her stay in Japan was almost over, and the next country was coming. This time it would be Hong Kong, a short visit with only two customers to see, which could be done in a day.

Eva landed in the incredible airport that is an artificial island, took a taxi to the hotel, and got prepared for the next day's meetings. As she did, she was texting again with Chris.

"So, next stop Hong Kong, quite a place, very old British empire, but quite a lot of local culture. South of China, Cantonese cuisine is just simply fantastic, some of the most praised food in the world."

Chris answered: "I have never been there, but it used to be the country with the Chinese contacts in the old times. Our company used to go through them to make parts. Now we go directly to China."

Eva wrote back: "Yes, I know, incredible, isn't it? It's such a small place. Everyone is very tightly packed together but very rich. I should go to Shenzhen, that is the next city in China, but I have no time this time. I'm not very keen on going there; last time I was there they offered me dog to eat, not something I do."

"Well, you are in China, love. They eat anything."

"So true, have you heard about monkey brains?"

"OMG that is disgusting."

"I know, some time ago I was invited in China to a very special dinner by a customer. There were not many people, and I didn't think much about it, we were in a special room and there were approximately seven people, at a round table, a special one with a hole in the middle. Well I thought it was going to be a typical Chinese hot pot, which I really like."

"Oh, what is that?"

"It is something very good. They put a pot with a special bouillon, I like the spicy one, in the middle of the table. Then they bring mushrooms, fish, shrimp, beef, chicken stomachs, noodles, and a lot of other things and you put them in the broth and cook them. When you think they are finished you put them on your plate, you add your sauces, and you eat them. The sauces are quite amazing, sometimes garlic, fish sauce, chili paste, there are many sauces you can chose."

"That sounds delicious. I always learn from you, incredible."

"Well on the evening I'm talking about, they came with a pot, but it was with a head of a monkey and the skull was open and it had been steamed. The eyes of the monkey were still moving. They placed it in the hole, and they were picking and eating at the brains. I just looked horrified at that picture and thought that I was in wrong movie."

"Wow, that is heavy."

"You bet. All of a sudden there was my customer who said, Eva, this is in your honor. It is forbidden now in China, but we could get it specially for you, please be my guest."

"Oooooo."

"Yes, I took a small portion with my chopsticks, I cannot even tell you how it tasted, I was so freaking shocked. Then they all came to me and started to toast with Chinese wine. It was the worst experience I ever had."

"Chinese wine? I have never heard."

"Oh, a typical Chinese horror, I think it is called *baijiu*, it is very strong, yellowish Chinese spirit. It has no taste, just alcohol. They toast in tiny glasses, but you have to *campai* everyone on them, meaning drink all in one go. In the beginning you look at the glass and you think I will survive, but after six of them, you know that you made the wrong calculation."

"Oh girl, I love you, you are just too funny."

"You make me blush."

The next day Eva visited her customers, who were typical stiff upper lip, British-speaking Hongkongers. Later in the evening she flew to Singapore; she arrived quite late and went to the hotel in a taxi. Singapore, Tokyo, and Hong Kong are the richest places in Asia, followed by Taiwan, and then there is China and the rest of poor Asia. The differences are incredible. Singapore is sometimes called the Switzerland of Asia because it is so rich and incredibly clean. It is quite common to see a Ferrari or some kind of extremely expensive and fantastic car. When the owners want to drive these cars at full speed, they go to the neighboring Malaysia, and they use the AH2 motorway, with some definite issues including hijacking. Singapore is a very strict place, though. The LGBT community is not really welcome, drugs are punished with the dead penalty, prostitution is heavily sentenced, and if you cheat in business you can get many years in prison. Singapore is a mixture of Indian and Chinese, and despite all the setbacks, the living is high and the food fantastic.

Eva related all of this to Chris in a text conversation. "Hi Chris, how is everything going in Florida? Just arrived in Singapore."

"Hi, was getting worried, had not heard from you for over six hours baby."

"Big part of that was customs and the flight."

"Here in Florida all is good, just dying to hear your stories again. When you get back to Switzerland I will come and visit you, baby."

"Oh, you are always welcome."

Eva's stay in Singapore was short but nice, with a Singapore curry crab dinner at the iconic Raffles Hotel. Next stop: Shanghai.

Shanghai's airport is probably one of the most modernized airports in the world and very organized. If you have a Chinese visa, it is fast and efficient to get into this country.

Shanghai and surroundings contain twenty-seven million people. It is a big and somewhat crazy city. This time Eva stayed in the center of Shanghai, in a western-style hotel. She stayed for the weekend and then for the week to see some customers in Nantong, Suzhou, and Wuxi.

Thunder had a factory in Suzhou, and most of the time she stayed there, but since she was there for the weekend, she managed to stay in the city center. During the weekend, she went to some incredible places, one was the Nanjing Xi Lu market, a fake designer goods market. It was the most incredible place. About ninety percent of this market was counterfeit, everything western that had a name brand, from watches to clothes, to luggage at one tenth of the price—and probably one tenth of the quality. One of the highlights of this market was a pearl shop visited by most important people in the world. One of the pieces that stayed in Eva's mind was a kind of knitted scarf made of real gold, with a gorgeous, big pearl on the end.

Well Nanjng road, Shanghai's shopping road is incredible, with one of the most unbelievable knife shops in the world, and the fantastic traditional silk shops. Yes China has an extraordinary history of arts and crafts and this is what one should search in this country, not necessarily the counterfeits. But as well the Yu Garden and the Tianzifang shopping area are remarkable places to visit, you will never forget them.

Some shopping centers in Shanghai are very luxurious, with all the best western names, and very expensive prices, some are specialized in very good Chinese names, very good fashion for somehow affordable prices, but just watch out for the sizes, Chinese people are usually smaller than western people so, try before you buy.

The center of Shanghai is truly incredible, and the growth unbelievable. One could go to Shanghai six months later and literally notice the difference, places ad even roads that were not there before. Unfortunately the growth is a lot to the cost of the local population that had to be displaced to other parts to give place to the different projects.

On one of her evenings in Shanghai, Eva went to a live music place near the Huashan Road. She had fun there and was always texting Chris about her adventures.

"Hi, gorgeous, another great evening. Unfortunately alone, hope next time it will be with you," texted Eva.

"Nice, what are you doing?"

"Just went to this place, they have a Filipino live band, great rock and western music. I really enjoyed it, but felt lonely."

"I can understand that. Yesterday I was in a bar with some friends in Fort Lauderdale, and you were just missing. You have to come here."

"Oh, yes, I will come and visit you."

"Anyway, I will probably have to go to Europe next week. When are you coming back home?"

"I am flying back at the end of the week."

"Perfect, I will coordinate accordingly."

Despite Eva's one incident with monkey brains, she found the food in China amazing; the variety and quality is just unbeatable. Yes, wherever you are in the world there is a Chinese restaurant, but that is adapted to the local taste. In China the food is quite different and the variety is extensive. In Shanghai you can eat everything that is Chinese or not Chinese; the typical Chinese dish from Shanghai are the soup dumplings. Near the city Temple in downtown Shanghai, there is one of the best known restaurants for this kind of food. Of course, Eva was there, too, and she even went to see the incredible amount of koi fish that are on the beautiful pond.

During her stay she was in a Korean-style restaurant where they served only tuna fish in all types of sushi dishes. The high point was to have bluefin tuna head sashimi, which was very expensive but incredibly good.

Later in the week, Eva came back to Switzerland, the usual twelve-hour trip.

Back home, it was time for a get-together with the girls. This time they met on a Tuesday evening after work in the Molino.

"Hi, Eva, back home again? One tour around the world, that must be very exciting! I've never done it," said Linda.

"Yes, it was quite a trip. On the business side I went to visit my customers all over, and it went very well. But this trip was somehow special. I met a guy in Chicago, he was having diner next to me, we started talking quite nicely. His name is Chris and he lives in Boca Raton, Florida."

"Oh, I know the city!" Victoria said. "It's north of Miami, I was there on my holidays."

"Nice to hear, I have never been there. Well, carrying on, you will never believe this, but the next day at the airport we met again, and we had a nice talk. He then went back to Florida, and I to Tokyo. The incredible thing is that we cannot stop texting with each other. Well, I grew quite fond of him, and I believe he of me. Now he told me he was arriving this Friday in Zurich, and he wants to spend the weekend in Basel. Apparently he has some business to do in Europe, not sure where."

"Wow, girl! Love is coming," said Olympia. "You are incredible some time ago you thought it was over, you were going to stay alone forever; now this time try to stay with him."

"Yes, but he lives so far away. I mean, Florida is not somewhere I can go for the weekend."

"You will manage. If you fall in love you will find a way to stay together," said Linda.

"You girls are so amazing. Thanks for the support. Anyway, you have to meet him."

"Oh, it's that bad? You already want us to meet him? Man, this is serious," said Victoria, and they all laughed.

"So, I have something special to tell you girls. I am moving to Zurich at the end of the month to live with David," said Olympia.

The girls started to clap their hands with joy for her.

"Oh, and when is the wedding?" asked Eva with a wink.

"Come on, sister, step by step. We're not sure yet; we will have to live together for a while before that happens."

"Oh, compared to you guys my life has been very quiet, just very active in bed. We are still trying to start a family, not many results so far," said Linda.

"Oh, sister, it will take a while. You have been on the pill for many years, and your body has to adjust, you know that," said Victoria.

"I know, it's a question of time, energy, and a lot of trying."

"Oh we are all sad for the trying," Olympia said sarcastically.

Victoria didn't share much about her life, but the others knew that she was still very much in love with her Lisa, but since there was no gay marriage in Switzerland, the only way for them to get together was to change her papers back to being a man, and that was very difficult. She had already had many issues getting her papers aligned with her preferred gender. The other option was for her to get married abroad.

The rest of the week went by like a rocket. Eva took Friday off to meet Chris, who arrived quite early from Miami. She met him at the airport.

"Hi, Chris, over here." She waved as he was getting out of customs into the arrival area. Chris saw her and went in her direction with a smile. Eva gave him her hand to shake, but he decided to kiss her on the mouth. It was a long and satisfying kiss.

"Oh," Eva said breathlessly. "Welcome to Switzerland, gorgeous."

"Thank you for picking me up. You have to tell me everything about this country. I've never been here before."

"Yes, I took the day off, will drive you to Basel, and then we have all weekend for ourselves. But you have to tell me, are you tired?"

"Well, a bit, but I could sleep well during the flight and I am in good shape. I just will have to rest a bit later."

"OK, since it is still very early for the hotel check in and you have never seen Zurich, I propose that we go to see the lake of Zurich, a very nice place. There is no lake in Basel; there we have a river."

Eva and Chris went to the Seefeldquai, parked nearby, and walked along the quay until they were in the restaurant kiosk. They were heavily kissing while they were there, and it was clear that they were a couple. Eva was enjoying herself a lot. After a short lunch she drove Chris to his hotel. He had a short nap, and Eva picked him up later in the afternoon. In the evening they went to a bar in the center of Basel and went out for cheese fondue in the famous Walliser Kanne restaurant.

"The most typical Swiss food is the cheese fondue," said Eva. "There are many types of fondue: Bourguignonne, that is with meat and a frying fondue pan; the Chinese, that is the Swiss version of the hot pot, usually done with beef and vegetables; and of course the chocolate fondue for dessert."

"Wow, that sounds very special. And what are you going to order today?"

"We will have a typical Swiss dinner. As a starter we will have *Bündnerfleisch,* this is dried meat from the east of Switzerland in an area called Bündnerland. It is very nice, after we will have a real Swiss cheese fondue. To drink we will have a Swiss white wine."

The waiter nodded and headed off with their order.

Chris drummed his fingers on the tabletop. "OK, I am ready, but tell me more about your lovely country."

Eva told him more about Switzerland, where she came from, and about her family. Chris told her about his family as well. Soon the fondue arrived.

"So I have to show you how to eat fondue. You see these special forks? Just put the bread on the fork and submerge it in the melted cheese. Just one thing: if you lose your bread you have to give a kiss to all the people at the table. Well since there are just two of us, you have to kiss me."

Chris understood very well, but he still lost a lot of bread and gave Eva a lot of kisses.

"Now with such a lot of cheese in your stomach, you have to have a schnapps. That is a strong Swiss alcohol. I have a very good Williams Schnapps at home; it is made from pears."

"OK, let's go. You are my guide," said Chris.

They arrived at Eva's house, she opened the door, and they came to the living room. Eva got two glasses and served the famous schnapps. They made a toast, drank, and started to kiss each other very intensely.

Chris took off his jacket, throwing it to the floor; Eva started to open the buttons of his shirt and kiss his torso. Chris grabbed Eva's breasts and massaged them; at the same time Eva took her blouse off and carried on working downward on her lover. She unzipped his trousers to see a very excited piece of equipment that she made even more exited with her mouth. Within seconds, they were both naked and enjoying each other. Eva got up, took Chris's hand, and guided him to her bedroom.

"Sorry my love, I have here some condoms, I think we should use them." Said Eva as she opened the drawer of her nightstand.

"Yes please." Answered Chris

This time she put him the condom and then added some lube.

They fell onto the bed and were soon making passionate love. They fell asleep in each other's arms, kissing and cuddling.

What Is Going On? Accept Yourself

The chemistry between Eva and Chris was real. There was an electricity between them that was very intense.

The next morning Chris was a little tired and jetlagged. Eva got up, made breakfast for them both, and brought it to bed. They started the morning by kissing.

"Good morning, gorgeous, did you sleep well?" asked Eva.

"Yes, my love, what a night. You are amazing."

"You were amazing, what a lover! So when do you have to go to your customer?"

"What customer—oh." Chris seemed kind of embarrassed. "I will tell you the truth: I only came for you, no customer."

Eva couldn't help grinning from ear to ear. "Oh, that is a compliment, my love. If that's the case, then we can go to your hotel now, get your things, and move you here in my house for the rest of the stay. I am not going to allow you to go away from me."

"You are so right, my love," said Chris, kissing Eva at the same time.

Eva was caressing his torso and smelling his manly skin and getting really horny again. This time Chris in a very nice way turned her and made passionate love to her. Again, like the rabbits, they were doing it again; she hadn't even had time to clean herself from the night before.

Oh my god, I am a real slut, thought Eva, though she loved every minute of it.

Sometime later they went to the hotel, got Chris's luggage, closed his account, and moved him to Eva's house.

They had a great time together, not only for the weekend, but Eva could took some days off work the following week to show her new boyfriend around Switzerland. They went to Bern, Zurich, Lucerne, and some of the touristy places.

In the middle of the week Eva started to have a lot of fear issues. She really liked this guy, and she had to come clean to him and tell him the whole truth. She took advantage of the fact that she was in the office that day to really think about what to do. Mr. Gorgeous came to pick her up from the office. As she got in the car, she was really nervous.

"Hi, my love," she told Chris.

"Hi, beautiful," he answered and they kissed passionately again.

"So, where do you want to go? Let's have a drink?" she said.

"Yes, wherever you want to go."

Eva took the steering wheel and drove them to Bruderholz. They stopped in the Wasserturm and left the car in a car park there.

"Let's walk, my love. I have something to tell you," said Eva.

"Really? So what do you want to tell me? Something shocking?"

"Yes, I have to tell you the truth about me."

Chris shoved his hands in his pockets. "What? That you were born a boy?"

Eva had prepared for practically every version of this conversation, but she hadn't prepared for this. She worked her jaw silently for a moment before she could say, "How do you know?"

"I was shocked the other day," he explained. "I was in the living room in the house and looking at your books. I thought it was somehow funny that you had so much information about transgender people. Then I opened one of the books to start reading and there was a dedication to an Emil wishing him a great transition to Eva. Then I started to understand. I couldn't believe it in the beginning, but somehow, I got it. I have been waiting since then for you to tell me."

"I am sorry."

"Sorry for what? That you are one of the most beautiful and incredible women I know? I adore you, and it really does not matter."

Tears sprang to Eva's eyes. "Seriously, you still love me?"

"For me you are a beautiful, sensual, intelligent woman; that is what I see. I never met you as a man, but you have to tell me all the details. Well, I have to say, sex with you is the best I have ever had and you have the right things in all the right places. I did notice that you have silicone implants, but that is not really unusual."

"I love you. You are the best man I have ever known." And she gave him a big kiss.

"And I appreciate the courage you had to tell me," he said. "It just shows I can trust you. Well, when I was going this through my mind I thought I was going through a bad dream, I was asking myself, 'Am I gay?' Then I thought about you and couldn't think of anything in you that is somehow masculine, so I am definitely not attracted to men, and you are for sure not one."

"What a relief!" Eva said. "I was having trouble sleeping because I didn't know how you would react when I told you."

"As you see, what has to be will be. No stress, just let things unfold as they have to. More importantly, I am going back this weekend; I have a company to run in Florida. But we have to plan your trip to Florida. I want to see you there as soon as you can come, love of my life."

This open, honest, and trusting conversation intensified the relationship even more. Eva told Chris everything about her youth and her struggles to become herself. They had long conversations and even longer lovemaking sessions.

One day in bed after a very intense love making session, Chris said, "I don't know what that doctor did your vagina, but he was certainly a master artist. Small enough and very warm and just delicious. I cannot even imagine what was there before; I don't really care either."

Eva answered him with a kiss and a whisper. "You are the best man in the world. I love you."

The weekend came too fast and Chris went back to Florida.

When he arrived he texted: "My gorgeous girl, my love, can't wait until you come and visit me here in Boca. Promise me you come as soon as you can, like tomorrow."

Oh, Eva would have given anything to go to Florida the next day, but at home things were getting complicated. In her job things were changing. A large shareholder of Thunder had decided to sell many of their shares, and there were new shareholders coming onboard. In the extraordinary board meeting, the new shareholders decided to replace Thomas as general manager of the company, and all of his employees were waiting for his replacement. It was not the right time to leave just then. Within a few days there was a large company meeting with all of upper management.

The finance manager started the meeting.

"Hi, everybody, I would like to introduce you to your new boss, Andreas. I already had some time with him, and you will get to know him soon."

"Hi, team. In the following days I will get to know you all better, I am sure, but I would like to present myself. I am your new CEO, so you have to help me a bit. First Switzerland is a new country for me, and second, I am a manager, not an engineer, so I am trying to understand what our products do."

Andreas was average height, slightly fat, no hair, a very white German complexion, blue eyes and glasses, was dressing a very formal dark blue suite with an open white shirt.

During all this time, Chris and Eva were video-calling for hours on a daily basis.

"Hi, my love, I really miss you. Please take the next flight to Florida," said Chris.

"Oh, I wish I could, but I just don't know what to do," said Eva. "Today, we had a management meeting, and the new CEO presented himself. He is German, doesn't know the Swiss dialects, and has never lived in Switzerland. That is not really an issue, he just has to deal with it. The rest is worse: he comes from finance, has no idea what we do, and he is managing a company that is all about engineering and very technical. We are all waiting to see what will happen. I cannot believe it. Thomas was in the company for over fifteen years. He was an engineer and knew the customers and what he was doing. Now God knows what will happen."

Chris frowned. "You see, love, that is what happens when companies go from owners to a corporation; you get these ridiculous managers that only care about how much they earn and no more about the health of their companies and their customers. Believe me, I know what the issue is."

"Next I will have a meeting with him. He wants to get to know me. I wonder if he already knows I am transgender. It is only a matter of time before HR will tell him."

"Don't worry, my love, just quit the job, come work with me, and we will make it a family business. It's the best thing; we will adopt some children, a real family, and nobody has to have anything to say about your past. Come to me, baby," said Chris.

Within the next few days, all of the management people had a meeting with Andreas, so eventually it was the time for Eva to meet him.

"Hi, Eva, I have heard a lot about you. You certainly are well recommended in this company," said Andreas by way of greeting. "Please sit down, and let's get to know each other."

"Thank you, Andreas."

"So tell me what you do here in a way I can understand."

"OK, I am an engineer and a saleswoman. I have been working for Thunder for the last ten years. I know the products quite well, the applications, I started with application technology of our machines, then I went to sales and customer service, then I was promoted to global sales dealing with key account management, and I support large international customers and do all kinds of other special jobs. Like I was ad interim manager for France, I did a lot of work to find a manager for China, and many other special projects. I speak many languages, travel too much for this company, and am more or less responsible for over twenty percent of the company's sales."

"Wow, that is impressive," said Andreas. "I understand you have a lot of knowhow, so please give me a list of your customers and what your budget is for them, or at least your strategy."

"Andreas, I thought you would ask that, so I have here a small presentation for you." Eva gave him a quite extensive presentation of her biggest customers, what were her action plans, and what she expected as the results. It was all quite well received.

"Well, Eva, I see that you know what you are doing. Can you arrange a visit for me to meet some of your main customers? I would like to meet them, but not too much traveling. I saw your traveling expenses. They are too high; we have to see what we can do about them."

"OK, I will arrange for some visits to France and England, that should not be too expensive. Let me know what dates I should aim for."

"I will send you an email with the details," said Andreas. "Thank you for coming in. I am sure we will work great together."

Well, that was Eva's initial contact with the new manager; she wasn't sure what to make of it. Later the same day she talked to Chris.

"Hi, love," said Chris. "Tell me, how did it all go with your new boss?"

"I thought it was all right, but I had some trouble communicating with him. He is like a wet fish, I cannot hold him, I don't have too much trust in him. He seems to want to know everything and then complains about my expenses."

Chris laughed at that. "He is just a finance guy leading an engineering company. Baby, you know what to do: take a plane to Florida and spend the rest of your beautiful life with me."

"Chris, baby, is that a proposal?"

"How many times do I have to tell you I love you?" said Chris.

"You are so cute. Love you too."

Some days later the girls were together again.

"What is going on with you, Eva? You have been completely absent from the group chat lately. Sometimes we don't even know if you are alive," said Linda.

"Oh my, oh my, oh my," Eva said. "Girls, life has taken a new turn. I honestly don't know where I am anymore. OK let's start from the beginning. Chris told me he had to come to Europe for a customer visit, but in reality he just came to see me. We had an incredible time together in all respects, sexually, intellectually, you name it. Well, he had to go back to Florida, and we have been texting, phoning, and video conferencing on a daily basis, and I mean for many hours a day. I cannot live without him anymore; he proposes to me more or less on a daily basis, and I am totally heartbroken. I need to take the first plane and go to him. I am totally in love."

"Oh my god, that is incredible! We are so happy for you, sister," said Victoria.

Olympia held up a hand. "Wait, Victoria. Eva, have you told him the truth? All the truth?"

Eva nodded emphatically. "Yes, girl, that was the most incredible moment of my life. I was so scared that he would dump me, but instead he did just the opposite. He simply told me he had found out about it and it didn't really matter. I am so in love with him and want to be with him, feel him inside of me. I am going crazy. I thought I could take some holidays to go see him, but guess what? The world changed in my company. Thomas left, and we have a new CEO, Andreas. I cannot place him yet; he is a real German in Switzerland, with no idea about our business, and a finance guy to boot. What a change from Thomas, who knew exactly what we were doing and was fair and respectful. I just don't know where everything is going with work, and it's keeping me away from Chris. I'm scared," she said.

"Oh, everything will be all right," Linda soothed her. "You'll see. Just trust yourself and follow your gut; it always tells the truth."

"Yes, give me a hug, Eva," said Olympia. "We love you. We all have difficult decisions to make sometimes. I can see one is just before you, but you know you will know what the right answer is."

"Eva, look on the bright side: you met the guy of your life. If that is not a sign, I really don't know what is, sister. What are you hanging on to? What is bygone is bygone; the only step is forward," said Victoria.

"Thank you, girls, I love you all," said Eva with tears on her face. "Enough from me, girls. Linda any news?"

"Why, I thought you'd never ask! Yes, I am pregnant. I took the test yesterday, and I was positive. I am going to be a mama."

All the girls just embraced her; they could not believe the happiness that that represented for her.

"Oh my god, we are all going to be aunts soon!" said Olympia. "I just don't have anything to share now, compared to your incredible changes and hopes. Sisters, I just love you."

As usual they had a great evening and were all so happy with these were big changes.

The day arrived for Andreas and Eva to visit some of her customers in Europe. The first flight was to Nice in the south of France; they were going to visit Eva's preferred customer, Mr. Mani.

Andreas flew business class and Eva economy. When they arrived in Nice, they went to the heliport, where a helicopter was waiting for them. A short car ride later, they were at the headquarters of the customer's company.

"Let me tell you welcome, Andreas," said Mr. Mani. "Nice to meet you."

"Thank you, Mani, Eva has told me a lot about you. I have seen that your company has bought a lot of stuff from us."

"Oh, that is because of Eva. She really has our engineers in her pockets. Although you are so expensive, you should give us a standard discount," said Mani.

"Oh, come on," said Eva. "You are taking advantage of the fact that Andera is here. Mani, I see you."

"Eva, I am talking with your boss, so keep quiet," said Mani in a joking manner, but Andreas didn't get it.

"Yes, Eva, keep quiet," said Andreas. "So, tell me, how is business going for you?"

"Thanks for asking. We have had our best year ever. You know I started very small, and these days I have a very big international company. I am not an engineer, but I tell you I tell our engineers how to run their machines. It has been always my hobby. You know, my secret is that I trust everybody, but see what you have to trust by controlling them, and it paid off. And that applies to my people and to my suppliers; when I met Eva, we had a big issues with Thunder. As a matter of fact we were talking lawyer to lawyer. Eva came here and we slowly sorted our problems out and resolved the issue. We both won, and we carried on our business. Unfortunately Eva has been too busy with everybody else and not us. But I can understand that."

The meeting with Mani was very interesting and positive for both sides. After lunch, they went back to the Nice airport and took a flight to London. This time Eva got an upgrade, and she was flying business in business class, though not next to Andreas. They had some time in Nice airport to chat before their next appointment.

"Well, that was a very interesting meeting with Mani. He is quite an impressive person, but I had an analysis of the business we did with him. The volume is quite high, but the margins can be better. We should increase prices with his company," said Andreas.

"Oh, you are not happy with the volume of business and profit?"

"Yes, I am, but I am sure we can improve."

"OK, I will try."

"Good. By the way, I was talking to HR about you. It was a very interesting conversation. I just want to let you know that I am a very religious person."

"Good, how can I understand that?" said Eva.

"Well, you are transgender."

"OK, and what else is there to understand? Are you going to fire me because I am transgender?"

"No, but I just want to state that I am very conservative and do not accept everything."

"OK, not sure what you mean, but I heard it."

That was the end of the conversation, and the rest of the trip was kind of icy.

That night, when they arrived at the hotel, Eva's first call was to Florida and Chris.

"Hi, love, so how was your trip to Monaco?"

"Quite incredible, next time I go there will be with you, to introduce your company, love. I think Mani will buy from you; you just have to prove to their engineering team that you have a first-rate product, and that I know you have."

"And what about Andreas?"

"Well, as he told me, he is a Catholic and transgender women are not really his thing. I believe my days are numbered in this place. Probably it is a sign from heaven that it is time to go to Florida to be with the love of my life. I really miss you. Tomorrow I am going to tell him that I have to go urgently to a customer in the US, and I will spend the week with you, cannot wait anymore."

"Now you're talking! Just let me know when you are coming. I cannot wait to have you next to me. Love you, my beautiful Eva."

The next day Eva and Andreas visited a customer in Croydon, next to London; the same afternoon they got back to Basel. On the way to Basel Eva told Andera that she had to see a customer in Schenectady, a very big one, and that she wanted to see a new factory near Miami of an existing customer. He did not really have a response, but seemed to approve.

The next day she booked the flights and arranged the meeting. One week later she flew first to Newark, taking the connection to Albany. She visited her customer in Schenectady and took the flight from Albany to Charlotte, and from Charlotte to Fort Lauderdale.

Chris was waiting for her at Fort Lauderdale airport. He was waiting for her at the entrance hall. The moment Eva saw Chris, her heart started beating like there was no tomorrow, and when their eyes crossed each other, there was a total meltdown in her head. Within seconds she found herself in his arms, and between there and bed it was just a complete, massive series of kisses, including while getting the luggage. They could not move away from each other; she didn't know where she was anymore. All she felt was the love and incredible attraction taking place between them.

When they got to Chris's house, they just had time to take the luggage out of the car, get inside, and go directly to bed. The rest of the day they made love with some short interruptions to drink champagne and have some snacks.

The next morning, they had breakfast together. Chris took her to his company and introduced everybody there, and in the evening they went for a fantastic Blood Mary and crab dinner at The Whale's Rib in Deerfield Beach, a really nice place. The rest of the week, they were simply enjoying each other as much as they could.

Chris's house was very nice, but somehow, the feminine touch was missing. She told him they would have to change this.

Boca Raton is a magical place in Florida, one hour north of Miami, it is the only place where the coast is not completely overtaken by skyscrapers. Boca has many university campus making it quite a young town in old age Florida. The history of this town goes back to the twenties, when a young Californian architect, Mr. Mizner made a hotel and golf course. At that time many new Yorkers had breathing issues because of the very polluted town that was heated by coal. So they went to Florida, mainly in winter. At the time there was no air conditioning and it was too hot and in summer too humid. During the second world war the hotel made by Mizner was taken by the air force and they constructed a landing strip, that was the training grounds of pilots of the bomber aircrafts against the Germans. With the invention of the air conditioner, Florida started to grow, from a small population to the third largest population in the US after California and Texas. Boca became the house of many famous people and a large Jewish community. Today Boca has some very large attraction like the Mizner Park. The old hotel became a Waldorf Astoria luxury hotel with tennis courts, golf courses, an incredible number of fantastic restaurants a beach house and all.

During her stay in Florida, Eva went with Chris to have dinner at Rosie's in Wilton Manors, about half an hour south of Boca. This restaurant was the second-most gayish place in the US, and transgender, gay, and lesbian customers are the norm there, together with the occasional straight person. Eva had never seen anything like that; she was impressed.

The trip to Florida made it clear to Eva that this was so much more than a fling. Going back to Switzerland was painful; Eva was totally puzzled over what to do, what to think. Her heart was in Florida; her mind and her constructive feeling were in another place that did not exist anymore. Thomas was gone, and Andreas could not be trusted. It was like opening the floor beneath her; she was somehow completely lost and falling ever deeper.

The final day of her trip arrived. She had to go back, and it would not be easy. She had stayed too long in Florida, and some people were not happy back in the office.

Miami to Zurich was the worst flight Eva had ever had. Sure, she was upgraded to business, the service and travel comfort were perfect, but her head was exploding. On one side there was what she always expected, a sense of continuity; she had worked so hard all her life to have a sense of security and strength. She had achieved it; she was respected, loved, and doing well. On the other side, all that had no meaning anymore. She was in love with Chris, and living without him had no meaning. All that she fought for all her life was gone, just like that. Life is just amazing, but sometimes what you plan for does not happen because there is some kind of entity that does not agree with it, God knows what. On the other side, what you dream and what you think will never happen can happen in a second, and you don't know how or why. On that flight she could not sleep. She was thinking, 'What shall I do with my life, love, stability? Well, is there anything called stability? Nothing is eternal.'

By the time she got to Zurich, the world was not clear, but she decided to trust herself.

She texted her Chris: "Just arrived in Zurich, miss you already. I know where I belong, my love. I will get everything ready.

Eva had one day to get herself together. She went to the office, sat at her desk, and it was not long until she was asked to go to Andreas's office.

"Hi Eva, can you explain to me where you were last week?" said Andreas.

"Sure, I was in Florida."

"OK, what were you doing there?"

"To tell you the truth I was there to visit my boyfriend and future employer."

"Sorry?"

"Yes, Andreas, I am leaving the company. So take this discussion as my resignation."

"What? Why are you leaving? Is it because I told you I didn't like transgender people?"

"Well, that certainly triggered it, but that is not the main reason. Let's say I had an offer I couldn't refuse somewhere else. Don't take it personally."

And she left the room.

Later the same day she posted her official letter of resignation and she phoned Chris.

"Darling, I am done. I'm coming home to you as soon as we can get this together. I gave my resignation here."

"That's my girl! When can you come, and I mean forever?"

"Help me. I have no idea how to come to you in an official way. According to Swiss law I have three months' notice, but I still have my holidays and overtime, so they will probably ask me to stay another two months—that is, if they want me to stay at all since I am in sales. Then we have to look how I can come to the US."

"No problem. You will come to work for me. Today I will get in contact with the immigration lawyer, and we will get things going. Please send me your CV, a copy of your passport, and if I need something else, I will ask you."

New Continent, New Life

It did not take long for Eva to get her confirmation that she could leave two months later. Thunder insisted that she stay and that she would assure a transition to a new person still to be designated. So, things were getting prepared.

At the same time Chris's immigration lawyer started to get all the paper together for an L1 Visa, since she was going to work for Chris's company as its international sales manager.

There was a lot to do: give notice to stop the lease of her house, pack boxes to send to the US, get the necessary permissions—and getting appointments at the US consulate is not necessarily an easy thing.

As usual the girls came together again, this time on the weekend.

"Girls, becoming a mother is quite nice," said Linda. "The hormones are making me strong, and I feel so good. I would recommend you do the same, I mean you, Olympia."

"Yes, I am jealous. That is one thing I will never be able to do, become a mother. But probably Lisa could. That would be great, to marry and have a child together," said Victoria.

"Yes, I want a child, too, but it will have to be adopted, or we could have a surrogate," said Eva.

"Yes, Eva! You have plenty of news. Come on, start talking," said Olympia.

"Well, life is definitely changing. What can I say? So, I am going to change continents. As you know I was in Florida with Chris, what a trip, it was the best in all possible things. I love him and don't want to be without him, so we had to make a couple of decisions. First, I am going to work for his company as sales and business development. Second, I am going to live with him in Florida. I already gave my notice to Andreas, anyway, this shit guy was telling that he was very Catholic, and he didn't like transgender people. It just came at the right time, as usual. So now I am preparing a lot of things, my visa to the US, the move, and of course sending all the information to my replacement. Nobody knows who that will be anyway."

"OK, I'm taking advantage of having you here in Switzerland now: I am having a party at my house in Zurich, just us and our partners. Saturday in two weeks, is it OK for you?" said Olympia and the girls confirmed.

They applied for the L1A Visa. Tech Dim, Chris's company, was mid-size and had a series of offices worldwide. They immediately got confirmation that the paperwork had arrived and was being processed, something that is very good but not really conclusive.

At work, there was a lot of talk and discussion. Most people knew that Eva was transgender and nobody had an issue with it, so when Andreas told everybody that he was very Catholic and transgender people were from hell, his new employees didn't really understand. Because Eva's notice came quite soon after Thomas left, this was not taken very positively for Andreas. Thomas was a beloved manager, and Andreas didn't really replace him. The labor market was very good for those looking for work, so of course, many people started to leave the company. It didn't take long before the board of directors started to notice that there was something that was not adding up.

About one month after Eva gave her notice, she received a telephone call.

"Hi, Eva, how are you doing? It's Alexander, the president of the board of directors for Thunder."

"Hi, Alexander, yes, I remember you at the meeting introducing Andreas."

"We hear you are going to leave the company after so many years."

"Yes, that is correct."

"May I ask you why?"

"Well, I have another opportunity at another company in the US," said Eva.

"I see, but is there any reason related to Andreas? Has he been a good manager?"

"Well, I have not had much contact with him lately, you know I am going and let me say not really interested anymore. Andreas is new in the profession, and he will have a lot to learn. And I am not sure if his beliefs and his culture will help him in the technical environment of Thunder."

"Oh, I see. You are not a fan of him."

"Not really, but Thunder will always be in my heart. We had a fantastic company; we built it with lots of sweat and love. I learned all I know here; it will always be remembered."

"I understand. So what are you going to do?"

"I am going to do the same thing I did here for a company in Florida."

"Oh, you already have a job?"

"Yes, they are securing my visa now to go to the US."

"Good luck with that. The US is a difficult place to go."

"Thank you, we are doing our best," said Eva.

In the next weeks the Thunder employees noticed Alexander's presence at headquarters.

The day came for the party at Olympia's place, and the Friday before, Chris arrived from Florida. Eva picked him up and took him home; she had to work, but was with him in the evening. They had not seen each other for some weeks and had a lot to catch up on. Being together was great as usual.

"Chris, since I am going to work for you in business development, and since I am bored to death but I still have to go to the office, can you send me the manuals for the Tech Dim machines, so that I can study them? I would also like some information about where we are present outside of the US. By the way, I just realized that many of my customers are potential customers for our equipment."

"Oh, I think I have the right person on board," he said with a grin. "You are already making plans! Of course, I will send you everything. We have to buy you a computer as well; I am sure your current computer belongs to Thunder."

"Yes, my love, but know that I am more interested in other tools too. Love you," said Eva, and she started to kiss Chris.

"By the way, I brought some presents for your friends, what do you think? I tried to get something based on what you told me about them. So, for Linda, I have two presents: one is some kid's dresses for toddlers, and the other is a beauty gift set from Burt's Bees for her to take care of herself. For Olympia, the sailor, I got a coaster set that looks like nautical ropes, and for Victoria, I got some roll-on perfumes. So what do you think?"

"Chris, I think you are going to be very popular with the girls. Just be careful, you are mine," said Eva, laughing and giving him a kiss.

On Saturday, they drove to Olympia and David's house in Zurich. It was a very nice place. Eva was really happy to be there. She was wearing a very nice red dress and some high heels, and feeling quite beautiful. She rang the door; Chris was behind her with the bag full of presents.

"Hi, Eva, hope you had a good trip to Zurich," said Olympia as she opened the door. "And this is Chris, I believe."

"Yes, you are right," said Chris.

"Well, Eva told us a lot about you, but she forgot to mention that you are so gorgeous. Good choice, girl," said Olympia as she directed them to the inside of the house.

Almost everybody was already there except for Victoria and her girl, Lisa, who arrived shortly after Eva and Chris.

After Olympia made the introductions, Chris said, "Hi, guys, it is so nice to see you all in person. I have heard so much about you, and I have to say Eva only told me the good things. It is really a pleasure to see you here. I have some presents as well, so I thought I would rival the great Swiss chocolates with some Floridian ones, and I have some small things: Linda for you, Olympia, and Victoria. Enjoy."

"Thank you very much," everyone said to Chris. He became an immediate star with all of Eva's friends.

"Now I would like to show you the house," said Olympia and then gave everyone a small tour .

They had a wonderful evening together, and they were all clearly interested in knowing more about Chris.

"Chris, Eva told us a lot about you, but we still have many questions," said Olympia. "So you live in Boca Raton, Florida."

"Yes, it is a very nice place, and by the way you are all welcome to visit Eva and myself there."

"Yes we were there this year for a short time on our way to Palm Beach, Lisa and I," said Victoria.

"Nice, I hope you liked it. I live near the intercoastal, the river that goes all the way from the north to the south of Florida. So every day I try to relax and walk to the beach; it's a fifteen-minute walk. You can come and visit us whenever you want. We have two seasons in Florida: the hot one and dry in winter and the hot and humid one in summer—well, and hurricane season."

"Yes, please be our guests. It would be great to see you," said Eva, kissing her knight in shining armor.

"What do you do, Chris?" asked Linda.

"I have a company that makes automatic measurement machines. Some are quite big and specialized. I have some factories in the US, and your friend is joining me in international sales. Yes, I think she can be a real positive asset for our company, with her knowhow."

"So you are a real entrepreneur," said Victoria.

"Yes, I suppose so. I had some ideas as a young man, after my studies, and I put them into practice. The rest came by itself. I used to live in another area, in Illinois, but then there was a nice opportunity to take over a company in Florida, and I decided to do it and made my headquarters there."

"Were you married before?" asked Olympia.

"No never, I was always too busy, but something fascinated me in Chicago about Eva. I never approached a woman like I approached her. And I don't regret it for one second."

It was really a nice and cozy evening. That night they were alone again in Eva's place. Chris spent the week in Switzerland, and they made many decisions about what to do, what to send to the US, and how to organize their life together.

The week after Chris left, Eva received a letter saying that she had to present herself to the US consulate in Bern. Incredible enough, it was two days after her last day at Thunder.

On the afternoon of her last day at Thunder, she brought in a cake, a lot of small things to eat, and some twelve bottles of champagne. She invited all her friends at headquarters to her going-away party, and there were over fifty people, more than half of the staff, there. They had a wonderful party; all her ex-colleagues were happy for her and wished her all the best. Sometime in the middle of the party Andreas arrived, opened the door, and came in. He got himself something to drink, and some minutes later he made some noise with his glass and started a small speech.

"Dear Eva, I am sad to see you leave. I understand that your private life is very important, and if I understood correctly, you are even changing continents to pursue your happiness and expectations. I would like to rise my glass to wish you a great future and that all your wishes come true. I am sorry if I was awkward and difficult; well, I have my beliefs as well. I wish you all the best, and I hope you'll think about us. We are losing a very important wheel of our mechanism. I just hope we can catch up. Thank you again for all these years you sacrificed for our company."

"Thank you, Andreas. Yes, I had a wonderful time at Thunder. I am leaving with some incredible memories of the people that helped me become the professional I am, the incredible education I got from them, but also the people that helped me through my transition, the people that helped me in this company, with their acceptance, love, and, I have to say, devotion. I will never forget them; they will be always in my heart. I have learned to become a good professional woman in this company, and nobody will ever take that away from me. I have to thank someone who is unfortunately not here, Thomas, for being patient, sometimes demanding, but mostly a very stable and fair boss. I know he is doing great; he has another very interesting job, a continuation of his amazing career. Anyway I thank you all for this amazing time."

Two days later Eva had an interview at the US consulate. They posed a lot of questions about her life, what she did, and what would be her added value for Tech Dim. In the end they told her all was OK and that she had to wait until she got the visa by post. Unfortunately they could not tell her the exact date.

Eva came back home, started packing, and getting things ready to go. The transport company came and packed up the whole house. In the meantime Eva was staying at Victoria's, for a couple of weeks. Then the requested document came, and it was time to go to the other side of the pond, to her new home. She took the first flight she could after giving all the papers and instruction for the container to the transport people.

In the end, Eva had to sell her fantastic Mercedes. For her it was a status sign that she had to give up; she placed an ad online and got a buyer very quickly. The transaction was made, and the car was gone. It was still a blow for her; that car had given her so many wonderful memories.

Finally the day came. She was flying from Zurich to Miami, and this time she was upgraded to business class on a one-way ticket. A good omen, she thought.

She sat at her place, 3A next to the window, which was ideal. She wanted to take some pictures from the sky, just to remember how wonderful Switzerland looked.

The flight went quite well, but she could not sleep. A new continent, new country, and new life were waiting for her. Her mind was going crazy with different thoughts.

On one side, I am so excited, being with this guy that I believe is my real twin mind, someone I trust and I love. I am so excited, but on the other hand, I am giving up my independence and the life I worked for. Well, that is exactly what so many cis women go through. And then there are many things connected with me being transgender. Well, at least there are no lies with Chris, and I have the opportunity to go into stealth mode in the US. Somehow there is a reason for everything in life, and one just has to follow what comes. I have to make a list of all the things that I have to do, my promotion concept for Tech Dim, oh so many things to do. But let's have some fun—what car shall I buy in the US? Well, I want an American car, either an SUV or a muscle car. Hmm, I always had a big love for the Ford Mustang. My cousin had one, and I loved it. Such an elegant car, a little pony.

The trip was a long one. She spent it thinking about her future, what was waiting for her, and about Chris. She was so happy to finally be with him again, this time for good.

When she arrived in Miami, Chris was waiting at the airport with a big car.

"Welcome home, my love," said Chris, kissing her. "How was your trip?"

"A long one. I could not stop thinking about everything, our future, so many things. Sometimes it's hard to know where to start. One thing I know, I love you."

"You will see, all will come step by step. Now, please enjoy the next few days. Be a tourist, go to the beach, get your stuff in the right place, and think about what you want to do when the container comes. Take your time to become a Floridian. I will introduce you to some friends, and step by step you will know everybody and then you can start with the company."

"Oh yes, it sounds like a good plan."

"We have to make sure that you have a car too. What do you want?"

"I was thinking about that. I'm not sure if I want a sports car or an SUV. What do you think?"

"A Ferrari?"

"No, I want a US-made car, a muscle car or an SUV. I like muscles..."

"Oh yes, a Camaro would suit you."

"What about a little pony, a Mustang?"

"Exactly, a convertible Mustang. That is the car for my girl. Love you, let's go and look at some cars tomorrow."

Eva and Chris arrived home, to Chris's house, where they would both live. It was quite a nice house as he showed her around, a Floridian home with about four bedrooms and a nice garden, but nothing spectacular.

"I think I know what you are thinking, my love," said Chris.

"Really?"

"Yes, you are thinking that you can rearrange the house to look more like you. And by the way you can do what you want to feel at home, just don't touch my office. Not for beauty reasons, but I still have a lot to do there."

"OK, you are a busy man, I can understand. I already love the house, I am sure we will make some changes, but with time," said Eva.

"And this is the backyard. I always wanted to have a pool but never managed to get it together. Probably you can work wonders with this outdoor space, my love."

After taking all of Eva's luggage in and having the excursion through the house, Chris and Eva went for a short rest—well, some cuddling and sex, they had to catch up. Afterward they went to a restaurant. Chris was a real Floridian; the fridge was almost empty and he never really ate home, always in the restaurant.

Yes, Eva thought, many things were going to change in that house.

The next day, Chris took Eva to a very special lunch.

"So, I want to introduce you to some of my friends and their wives. We are going to have lunch together with them." Chris drove them to a very nice restaurant called Farmer's Table. Eva was dressed very casually; after all she was in Florida. She had on brown shorts and a white jersey top and some beige wedges.

When they arrived, four people were already waiting.

"Hi, everybody, let me introduce you to Eva, the love of my life," said Chris. Eva smiled. "And this is John and his wife, Ellen, and Shawn with his girlfriend, Brenda."

"Hi, so nice to meet you," Eva greeted everybody. "Chris has talked very highly of you."

"Let's go and sit and drink something, but we have to know all about you, Eva," said Brenda.

They sat down and ordered some aperitifs and starters.

"So, you are from Switzerland we heard," said Shawn.

"Yes, I am from a town called Basel in the north of Switzerland. It borders Germany and France."

"Yes, I was there once. It is famous for its pharma industry, right?" said Shawn.

"Correct, and some very good engineering companies," said Eva.

"Yes, I remember, I was there with another company that does some things for the electrical industry. Then we went to Zurich, also a very nice place," said Shawn. "And of course well known for its banks, and having issues with the IRS."

"You are right, said Eva, laughing

"And tell me, what did you do in that beautiful country?" asked Ellen.

"I was an international sales and business development woman, working for a large company dealing with special equipment," said Eva.

"Nice, so will you be helping Chris in his company?" said Ellen.

"Yes, Eva will be working with me, but first she has to get used to Florida and make herself at home. She does not know many people yet; I think you guys are the first."

"Oh yes, you just arrived! You have to get to know this place; there is a lot to do," said Brenda. "You have to give me your number. We should go shopping together; I will introduce you to all the good places around here."

Eva was off to a good start with Brenda and Ellen.

After lunch, Eva and Chris went to see some cars. They looked at some Mustangs, some Ford Explorers, and they went to see some Camaros and Corvettes as well. Eva was not sure what she wanted after looking at all of the cars, so they decided to rent one for a week or until she got a permanent one.

The next day Chris went to the office. Eva got up a bit later, and she started to look at the house, every single room one after the other. Then she picked up her rented car; she was lucky and got a Ford Mustang, upgraded.

In the afternoon, Brenda and Ellen invited her to a small get-together. Brenda picked her up from the house, and they drove to Mizner Park, a beautiful place with a park and fountains, two roads and housing and shopping, restaurants, and at the end of the streets there was a recreation area, where many shows take place. It was a beautiful, high-class place. They sat at a bar outside and ordered some dry martinis.

"So, you do have a lot of work until Chris's house feels like home. He is a workaholic, no time for his own house," said Ellen.

"I think you are right, but I think Eva will get it all together. She is very capable," said Brenda.

"Thank you, girls, but I am going to need your help. Please give me some tips on where to find painters and gardeners and furniture... I am a bit lost, never have done this in the US."

"Yes, we will give you some tips. Just text us and we will tell you what to do. By the way, do you already have a US phone?" asked Brenda.

"I should get it shortly. Chris is organizing it for work; as you know we are going to work together," said Eva.

"Yes, we heard, that will be interesting," said Ellen.

They talked a lot, and afterward they went to look at the various shops, including a very nice furniture shop. After that Eva went to Publix, a supermarket and bought a lot of food to make dinner and have some nice wine. She went home and started getting the kitchen and refrigerator organized.

Chris texted: "Almost finished, what food do you want to go and eat tonight?"

Eva answered: "My love we are eating at home, I will serve you and then you can have me as dessert. Love you."

"Wow, that is a surprise."

When Chris came home, there was a great spaghetti dish with shrimp and a pesto sauce. It was really good, and Chris was astonished.

"I think it is the first time for a long time that I have eaten at home. That was incredible."

"Thank you, my love. I am sure you will get used to it."

"I really liked this."

"Question: Do you think that it would be all right if I painted all the walls in white, inside and outside? It gives a better, lighter house. Some of the colors inside are very heavy, and I really don't like the color in my office."

"I think it is a great idea. I never changed the colors in this house. They have been the same since I bought it, and it's true some are really dark and heavy. Go ahead get a quote. There is this website that can help you find the right people. The other one to look at is Craig's List." He wrote both names on a piece of paper.

The next morning, Eva did her research and booked three different painters to have look at the house to make a quote. At the same time she started to see about decorations, what she had that could be used nicely, and the colors and decorations for the individual rooms. The first painter came the same day and took all the measurements for the quote. Some days later Eva presented Chris with the quotes of the three painters. The differences were quite large, but they agreed on the one to take. It was the beginning of a big change in the house; with all of these changes, it would look prettier.

When Eva's packing container arrived, she took her things out. Most of her furniture was put in the right place, and she bought some other furniture and decoration to make things perfect. She always was in contact with her two new friends. She wanted to have a feel for the American taste, as well as some friendly advice, and she got both all the time.

"Oh my God, I am coming home today, and I cannot recognize where I live anymore. But you know, love, I like it more now than before. You have done a great work, love it," said Chris to Eva as he came home one day.

"Thank you, darling. Let me know if there is something that I have to change."

"No, all good. I love it. You certainly have taste."

She also made the decision to buy a white convertible Mustang. She didn't want Chris to pay for it, it was hers, so she managed to get a quote from Ford and get a list of things that she needed to buy the car. There were some small issues: she needed proof of residence and a bank account. It seemed there were many things to do to get settled in the US. She started to do them all one by one. It took a couple of weeks to get a bank account, social security number, and driver's license. When she had it all, she went to the car dealership and got herself her white Mustang, brand new, with a leather interior. Immediately she brought back her rented car.

The evening she got her car, Chris came home and asked how her day was.

"Nice, many nice new things, and a lot of work at home. What about your day, my love?"

"Busy, busy, I cannot wait until you start to work with me, but please take your time."

"You know I could start to work half days until the house is organized and then go full time. What do you think? I want to start working with you as well."

"That is a great idea. By the way did you get a new car from Avis?"

"No, I just brought the old one back today."

"But there is a brand new Ford Mustang in front of the house."

"Yes, I know, isn't it nice? White with a black sun roof?"

"It certainly is, just like the one you wanted when we were at Ford."

"I know, and now it's my car," said Eva.

"What? Did you buy it?"

"Sure, yes I did."

"How did you pay for it?"

"Money, my love."

"You paid cash?"

"Yes, love, I did. It's our car; you can drive it whenever you want." And she kissed him.

"You are an emancipated girl! I love you."

The next Monday, she started to work at Tech Dim. In the morning she came for the first time to the weekly meeting with the company's management team.

"Hi everybody," said Chris. "Welcome to the Monday meeting. I hope everybody is doing OK and had a nice weekend. Before we start, I would like to present you all to a new person in this company. Her name is Eva, and she is going to do business development for us. Eva is from Switzerland; she speaks a multitude of languages and has been to many countries. She used to work for a company in Switzerland that did special testing equipment; she was key account manager taking care of large customers globally. Please help her feel welcome and at home."

"Welcome on board," said a woman who introduced herself as Betty. "Nice to see a girl in sales." The rest of the crew followed with hellos.

"OK, let's start the meeting. Nick, your news and action plan."

Eva started to get integrated into the team. On the second week, she went to see some customers with Nick, the sales lead. She was learning, but it was not a difficult subject for her. Within two months she had her first sales, and she was starting to acquire new customers, mainly from past customers she brought with her from Thunder.

As she started to work, she had less time for her new friends, so they decided to make a kind of regular girls' night. The three couples would also get together quite often, for dinners, sometimes in boats, going out to sporting events together. There was always something to do in Florida, and Eva was getting very well integrated.

Soon, though, she was going to Europe to visit customers and of course her friends. One Friday, she flew to Basel and had dinner with the girls.

"How long have we not been all together? You are beginning to be a stranger, Eva," said Linda. "Look at my belly: you are going to be an auntie very soon, you know."

"Yes, and it is going to be a boy! You must be so happy," said Eva. "You still have not told us what his name will be."

"Yes, I am very happy for Alex. The room is ready, and in three weeks I will be a mom."

"We are so proud of you, Linda, a real mom! I love the name Alex for Alexander," said Olympia.

"Yes, I agree," said Victoria.

"I am sure I will not be here for the birth of your son, but you will be on my mind, sister," said Eva. "So proud of you."

"And how have you been in Florida?" said Linda.

"Quite good. Chris is a real gentleman. I redecorated the house for him, gave it some new paint, some of my furniture, some new things, and the house just feels and looks fantastic. And I got a Ford Mustang, and am working with Chris. But I certainly miss you girls, even if we are always texting. When are you coming to visit me? We have a guest room."

"Well as a matter of fact, David and I were thinking of coming sometime at the beginning of next year, during the season," said Olympia.

"Can you take a second couple?" said Victoria.

"Yes, I can transform my office into a second guest room," said Eva.

"Come on, you will visit from time to time, and we will always stay in contact," said Linda. "For me and my kid it will be too early to travel. I wish I could, but it will not be possible for a little while."

Is There an End or Just a New Beginning?

Eva came back to Florida, where Chris was waiting impatiently for her. Some weeks later Linda had her Alexander. Eva sent her a huge bouquet of flowers and of course a huge selection of boy's clothes and toys from the US. They had an internet party together. Linda was so happy, and the girls were loving her new life changes.

Victoria, Lisa, Olympia, and David came to Florida. Eva took some days off to show them around; they went to see all the iconic tourist places: Miami Beach, Bayside, the art district, Little Havana, did the obligatory Everglades alligator tour, Fort Lauderdale, Palm Beach, and took some time to go to Key West and Orlando to enjoy Disney World and Universal Studios. They had a great time.

One of the last days of their trip was reserved to go shopping. It was a must, Eva said, to go to the Sawgrass Mills and get some of the incredible deals they had to offer. As usual, they started by buying a big suitcase, and filled it in every shop with clothes, shoes, sports items, gifts to take to friends and family all at incredible prices. They started very early and were there until the mall closed. Olympia had to buy a second suitcase, the first was already so full.

The last night they all went to have dinner in Wilton Manors at Rosie's.

"Well, I am so sad to see you going. I wish you would stay longer with us," said Eva.

"I know. We loved being here. We can see that you really live in an incredible paradise, really nice," said Lisa. "Victoria and I were once here in Wilton Manors. We had a great time dancing in a lesbian bar. Anyway, thank you for taking us here."

"Yes we loved it here too. I was a bit disappointed because I did not see many sailing boats, most of them are big stinkers, but being so near the Caribbean, I am sure that there are many of them," said David. "It would be great to have a second house here with a boat."

"Yes, just remember that here there are property taxes, and for boats, the issue is the hurricane season, if you are in Switzerland and the bad weather is coming you have to displace the boat somewhere safe. It is always a question of costs and availability." said Chris.

"I like your idea, my love," said Olympia. "We could come here regularly then."

"You know there are many people here that only come for the winter season. We call them snow birds. Most come from Canada, or the northern states of the US, but I know that there are some Swiss people, well mostly pensioned people."

"Wow, that is a great idea," said Olympia. "Unfortunately I cannot work from a computer. It would be very difficult, but probably one day things will change."

"I am so glad that you guys liked your visit. I'm still missing Linda, Frank ,and of course Alexander. I cannot wait to meet the little guy," said Eva.

"Yes, he is so cute, still very small. We now have our get-togethers in Linda's house because she cannot come to the restaurant, but we miss you a lot," said Victoria.

They had a great dinner in the garden of the restaurant; the evening had a fantastic temperature and great weather. The next day Eva's friends packed and in the afternoon they left for Miami for the flight home. They had so much luggage that they had to bring a pickup from the company just for the luggage.

Eva was sad that they left, but life was quite good for Eva and her Chris. They both worked for Tech Dim, but they were not always together. She traveled a lot, almost as much as before with international sales. After one year, Chris made her international sales manager, still working for Nick. She was very well integrated into the company, and everyone loved her a lot, and were proud that she had brought so much business to the company.

One day she was visiting a customer in Costa Rica when she got a text from Chris.

"Hi love, how is your trip going?"

"Great, customer is buying one machine and is probably going to buy another for his shop in Chile."

"Nice. I like that. Question, you are coming today home, you have a flight at 4pm, is this still correct?"

"Yes, I will make it for that flight," wrote Eva.

"Please do me a favor, when you go to the airport text me."

"Sure, my love. Will do."

When she left the customer and took a taxi to the airport, she texted: "Leaving now, will be at the airport in twenty minutes."

"Perfect, please go to door A at departures."

She told the taxi driver where to go. When they arrived at the airport, she almost got a shock seeing Chris at the airport waiting for her. She was leaving the taxi when he intercepted her and got inside the cab. He told the driver, "Please go to this address," and handed him a piece of paper.

"My love, what are you doing? Why are you here?" asked Eva.

"Well- I had to make a last minute trip to the region, so I decided to come and get you."

"You are full of surprises, I didn't expect to see you here. But I think I am going to miss my plane," said Eva.

"Don't worry, my love. I have it all under control, just trust me."

"You know I do." And they kissed. Very soon they were in front of a very small, private terminal.

"Wow, this looks like a private plane."

"Almost, chartered," said Chris. They paid the taxi and entered the terminal. They went to a kind of customs where they showed their passports, and on the other side they got in a very luxurious car that drove them up to a small Learjet.

"Wow, we are going home in style," said Eva.

"Yes, we are, just you and me."

The luggage was placed in the jet and they entered the luxurious plane. Eva was stunned. The airplane had two pilots, and one of the pilots was also working as their attendant.

"Welcome, Eva, welcome, Chris. Are you ready to go to Boca?" said the co-pilot.

"Sure! Wow, I cannot believe this. Such an incredible machine, and so great and beautiful. Look at those chairs! This is comfort," said Eva.

"Yes, baby, I hope you like it," said Chris.

"Why did you do this? I would never have believed it if you told me."

"Well, a customer arranged it. It's a long story, though. I will tell you afterward."

The plane took off, and the pilots made a short detour so they could see the city and a bit of the Pacific Coast of Costa Rica, then they got onto the right course and to the cruising altitude. Then the co-pilot came out and brought a bottle of champagne in a cooler, two glasses, and a small plate with cheese, cheese pastries, and grapes. He served the champagne and said, "Enjoy," and went back to the cockpit.

"My love, I raise this glass to our happiness and future," said Chris, getting up and sitting on his armrest to look at her.

"Oh, I love you, this is so nice," said Eva as Chris approached to kiss her.

They had kissed for a very nice minute, when suddenly Chris said, "Oh shit, can you help me? Something just fell down." Eva got up and started to look at the floor. She immediately saw a small box, and without thinking twice, she got it from the floor and gave it to her lover. He took it from her hand and opened it. It was a blue jewelry box with gold ornaments, and what was inside made Eva almost jump.

"Wow, this is beautiful," said Eva.

"Yes, baby, it is yours, with one small question: Would you like to spend the rest of your life with me? Would you like to be my wife, my lover, and the person I share everything with?"

Eva was speechless. She leaned into him, gave him a very strong kiss, and all of a sudden she was shaking. Her eyes were dripping with tears, and her heart was running wild. "Yes, please, I love you."

Chris took the ring and placed it on her finger. Eva had a glimpse at that incredible solo diamond ring—at least two carats, just stunning—before she carried on kissing her fiancé . Well, they were alone, and they started to get really horny. Eva trailed her fingers down his torso and slowly touched a very stiff member. She almost automatically went on her knees, opened his trousers, giving freedom to his cock, and kissed it passionately. Chris started breathing heavily, and Eva took off her underpants underneath her skirt. Within a couple of minutes Chris was lifting Eva up. She went with her knees on top of the seat and he approached from behind her and penetrated her. They had beautiful sex together, an experience that would remain with them for life. After sex, they were kissing and hugging.

"Love, my wonderful man, I need to know something: Do you want to have children?" said Eva.

"Yes, I do. I think it would be fantastic, but the question is, do you want to as well?"

"Yes, I do. To have a child from you is so important for me, to have a real family. But you know I cannot get pregnant. I think we should find a surrogate after our wedding. That way, it will be our kid made with your genes."

"I love you, but first let's prepare for our wedding," said Chris.

Eva could not take her eyes off that gorgeous diamond ring, which was now hers. She wasn't sure what she had done to deserve this, but whatever it was, she thanked God for this stroke of luck.

Soon they started to approach Boca Raton. The co-pilot came in, and they sat in their respective chairs.

"You look like you had a good trip. We will land soon, so let me clean up," he said.

They landed in Boca Raton and went directly to the Yard House, a restaurant in Mizner Park.

Their friends Ellen, John, Brenda, and Shawn were waiting for them.

"Hi guys, where have you been?" said Brenda.

"Hi troops, sorry, we just arrived from Costa Rica, and the customs took longer than expected," said Chris.

"Oh, that is incredible. So you just landed in Miami?" said Shawn.

"Oh no, we just landed in the Boca Raton airport."

"But that's only for private jets," said Shawn.

"Correct, we just had a very special trip," Eva said, showing him her finger with the gorgeous ring. "One we will never forget."

"Yes, I just proposed to Eva," said Chris.

"And I said yes," said Eva.

Everybody went totally crazy, congratulating the newly engaged couple. The congratulations were flying, and with some cocktails, it was quite incredible.

"So when are you going to get married?" asked Ellen.

"I believe quite soon, we have to get it all organized."

"Any thought on where are you going to do it?" asked John.

"No, it's still too early, but we are thinking and will start organizing it," said Eva.

They had a great evening. The next morning Eva was in front of her computer calling her best friends from Sweden.

"Hi, girls, how are you doing?" said Eva.

"Doing great, wish I was in Florida. Here in Switzerland the weather has been very bad," said Victoria.

"Me too. By the way, we are getting ready with that project to buy an apartment in Florida," said Olympia.

"I am still swimming in diapers. Little Alex is getting very big and strong, but I am so happy. I hope one day you all have one," said Linda.

"Nice to hear. I have a very important question for you. When can you all come to Florida?" asked Eva.

"Why should we come to Florida? I think I could travel with Alex , but it has to be an important reason," said Linda.

"Well, I cannot get married without my best friends," said Eva. "It's just simply not possible."

"What? Did I hear right? You are getting married?" said Victoria.

"Yes! Chris asked yesterday. He picked me up with a private jet and he proposed during the flight. It was in every way a memorable day." She showed the ring to her friends.

"Oh, wow, you are a lucky girl," said Olympia.

"Sure, I will come," said Linda, "with Alex and Frank. You tell us when and we will coordinate it with our work."

"We will get it organized as well," said Olympia.

"Lisa and I as well, we will find a way. You know Eva, I always wanted to get married to Lisa. If she is OK with it, we could get married at the same time, kind of a back-to-back wedding. Would you be all right with that?" said Victoria.

"Oh, I will be the only single one then?" said Olympia, and they all laughed.

"Ok, let me see how we can organize that. I will look into it and keep you posted," said Eva.

It was going to be a special day, two weddings, one straight and one same-sex. It was going to be a very unusual wedding day with three brides and one groom. There were many discussions among the four of them until they made a decision to do it. Lisa was enchanted by the idea, and both Eva and Victoria were such good friends. Chris was the usual great gentleman; he always proved to be someone special.

Eva found a great place for the wedding, a beach resort with a great restaurant and enough space for about 250 people. Both couples thought they would have about two hundred people altogether, meaning about forty for Victoria and Lisa and some hundred sixty for Eva and Chris. The issue with this place was, of course, the date. They were lucky and got a date within four months, on a Saturday evening, and they booked it.

The next challenge was to find an officiant for that date, and with some challenges. On one side there was a trans straight marriage, even though most people in Florida didn't really know that Eva was trans; on the other side there was a trans lesbian marriage. No religion would be the best, for all parties concerned, so some sort of mystical person would be their best bet. After looking they found a person that would be fantastic; they had a FaceTime discussion and they decided on her.

Eva had called her parents and even with all the issues between them, they were going to come to the wedding; they wanted to meet her husband and after many discussions, Eva's father agreed to give her away. Somehow they promised not to misgender her. Chris's parents were coming along with his uncles and very big family. In the end they were about two hundred people.

Eva went to choose her dress with Ellen and Brenda at a shop called Boca Bride. The first dress she chose was an ivory sheath dress fitted through the hips with a flared silhouette and sweeping train, and a deep V-neck. It actually fitted her very well.

"So, girls, what do you think," said Eva.

"I like the color, but I think the dress is way too simple for you. You deserve something more dramatic, and don't forget, you will be with two other beautiful girls, and you have to look even more glam," said Ellen.

Brenda nodded and snapped a picture of the dress.

"OK, let me try the next one." Said Eva. Some minutes later she came out in another ivory sheath wedding dress, this time in embroidered tulle with a sweetheart neckline and open back. The train was not too long.

"Oh, I have to say, that looks more like you, but I am not sure that your silhouette is so well done," said Brenda.

"Oh, I don't know. I like it," said Ellen.

"Please take a photo, and I will try another dress."

Eva came out in a third dress. It was a very light ivory ballgown with visible boning details, removable sleeves in embroidered floral appliques that also went down the tulle skirt. It was quite an incredible gown.

"Oh my god, this looks incredible on you," said Brenda. "I like it the best so far."

"I like it as well. Let me take some photos and send them to my friends in Switzerland to see what they say, but it is almost a yes to the dress. I just have to look at the accessories and mainly the shoes," said Eva.

Eva sent all the pictures to her friends and mainly to Victoria and Lisa. They all agreed on the third dress. Eva also got to see the dresses of Victoria and Lisa. Victoria would be wearing a beautiful white lace sheath dress with a short train and a sweetheart neckline, and Lisa would be wearing very feminine white loose trousers and a top with a crystal diamond belt. They looked amazing.

Eva, Victoria, and Lisa decided the bridesmaids were going to all be in a kind of sandy beige color. There was Linda, Olympia, Ellen, Brenda, and two friends of Lisa's, so they did not have the same dress just the same color.

The day of the wedding was getting closer, but there were still so many things to organize, like invitations, gift lists, hotels, and flights, really a lot.

Chris had a stag party with his friends and the three wedding girls has a bachelorette party about two days before the wedding. The girls went to Lips a very well-known drag show in Wilton Manors quite late in the evening. The issue was that there was that were quite a lot of lesbians in attendance, so they preferred to see girl strippers and the others were straight and they preferred male strippers.

The night before the wedding they had a special dinner just for Eva's and Chris's direct families. It was a very interesting evening; they laughed a lot and all had a great time. But Eva was thinking, 'Thank God my parents are not so good with the English language and the people here understood that. They misgendered me at least ten times, and nobody noticed.'

Finally the day of the marriage came. The girls got ready and made a party out of it. They had two hair stylists and a make-up artist come to Eva's house. Chris to his best man's house; there were too many women in his house, he joked, and, well, it was quite a lot going on. Linda's son Alex stayed with Frank at the hotel.

"Get the bridesmaids ready before us," said Eva to the stylists. "We will probably take longer, and they can help us get dressed afterward."

"Yes, that is a good idea," said Victoria.

"So, you girls are getting a double wedding. Are you going to a double honeymoon as well?" asked Linda.

"Oh, come on. We are friends but not like that; we'll have separate honeymoons," said Victoria.

"And where are you going?" asked Olympia.

"For the moment we are staying in Florida. If I lived here I don't think I would ever go on holidays again. This is paradise already, so beautiful," said Victoria.

"We decided not to go on honeymoon," said Eva. "We are going to have an exhibition for the company in Shanghai, so we are taking a week off in Phuket after the exhibition, that will be our time off. But we are giving ourselves a wonderful wedding present: we are building a swimming pool, with a jacuzzi of course."

Before they knew it, it was time to go to the venue. They went to the cars, two made-up Rolls Royces. The car with only bridesmaids in it went first, and both wedding cars drove to the beach resort. The car with Lisa stopped first in front of the main door. Lisa and the girls left. All three fathers were waiting at the door, and as Lisa came out her father took her. The next car arrived, and the respective fathers took their daughters. One of the girls from the resort told them that they could go in, all was prepared, and the ceremony began. The first to go in was Eva and her father, followed by Lisa and Victoria, who went at the same time. All the guests were already seated and waiting. There was a beautifully decorated arch, and in the middle was the officiant that was going to marry them. On one side Chris was waiting for Eva. Next to Chris was his best man, and the bridesmaids distributed on both sides. Eva's father gave her to Chris and went to his seat. Then the two other brides came at the same time with their fathers.

When all were in place the officiant started. "Welcome, everybody, we are all here together to celebrate a very unusual but very lovely ceremony. We are marrying two couples, Eva to Chris and Lisa to Victoria. We will marry one couple after the other, but for both couples I would like to make a small speech. Love is love, and it does not matter who, where, when, or why. Two couples are here to commit themselves to love, to help and share each other forever in the name of marriage. It is your most valuable treasure. Love is not jealous or boastful or proud or rude. It does not demand its own way. It is not irritable, and it keeps no record of being wronged. It does not rejoice about injustice but rejoices whenever the truth wins out.

Love never gives up, never loses faith in each other, is always hopeful, and endures through every circumstance. I will start with Lisa and Victoria. You have chosen to write your vows and express your binding promises of love, honor, and cherish one another. If you are ready to make these promises to each other, I invite you now to face each other and declare your intentions. Who would like to go first?"

"I, Victoria, take you, Lisa, to be my wife. I promise to be true to you in good times and in bad, in sickness and in health. I will love you and honor you all the days of my life," said Victoria.

"I, Lisa, take you, Victoria, to be my wife. I promise to be true to you in good times and in bad, in sickness and in health. I will love you and honor you all the days of my life," said Lisa.

"Thank you for sharing your vows with all of us. The rings you are about to place on each other's fingers are symbols of the love you expressed. They will remind you of the vows you have just spoken, and of the eternal love that you have for one another," said the officiant. Chris's best man gave the rings to Victoria and Lisa, and they placed them on the correct fingers.

"By the power given to me by the American Marriage Ministries and by the State of Florida, I now pronounce you wife and wife. You may kiss your bride." They kissed each other, and there was a general smattering of applause.

"Well, since we have a double marriage, we are now going to marry Eva to Chris." She proceeded to do an identical ceremony with Eva and Chris. In the end they exchanged the rings, kissed, and there was more applause.

"Well, that was a first for me to do a double wedding," said the officiant. "I wish you all a great evening."

The two couples came together ."Victoria, Lisa, I wish you all the best for the rest of your life," said Eva. "You will always remain very special in my mind no matter what happens."

"Chris, Eva, I can only repeat your wonderful words," said Victoria, her dear sister. "I love you and thank you."

Next came a never-ending session of photos with family, friends, and many other guests in an exhausting amount of combinations.

Finally they were all sitting at the tables, eating, drinking, and having fun. Very soon came the toasts and speeches. Olympia and Linda made a fantastic presentation with pictures of the girls together, from holidays to birthday parties, and they gave a very funny and motivational speech. Chris's best friend and his father also gave great speeches.

After the dinner there was a band playing and the floor was open for the party. The two couples opened the dancing, and soon they would be followed by many of their guests.

It was a lovely evening. Later that night Eva said to Chris, "I never thought I deserved such a wonderful partner like you, my love. You are the most incredible person in the world. You proved to me that you are understanding, a real gentleman, a very shrewd and good businessman, and an incredible lover. What else can a person ask for? I love you." They shared a long and very intense kiss, started to cuddle, and grew into hot lovemaking, a night they would never forget, with a lot of kisses, cuddles, and deep, missionary-style love.

The next morning, Chris woke up first. He stared at the still-sleeping Eva and hugged her from behind until she woke up.

"Hi, love, already awake?" she asked.

"Yes, my love, I could not sleep. We really had the most magnificent wedding I thought possible. I must say this double-wedding thing gave it a kind of a boost as well."

"I know. Everything was well done and prepared. You looked magnificent in your tux."

"Well, you too, love of my life. You were the most beautiful bride in the world. A new life for us." He gave her a deep kiss. "Well, Eva, I had to dream about children. Are you still OK with finding   a surrogate to have our child?"

"Sure, we already talked about it, so let's find one. I want to be mother."

"Yes, let's do that," Chris said. "I will have to go to the sperm bank for the insemination as well."

"What? No, my love, we will get one where you can put your semen directly into her. I think that is much better. That way, you will know that you did it."

"You mean you want me to have sex with this woman? A stranger?" He ran a hand through his hair. "Christ, Eva, we just got married.

"Of course, my love. I am just so sorry I cannot give you any children," said Eva.

"OK, but only on one condition!"

"Oh, you are asking for conditions? Why?"

"Because I love you, and I want you to be present for that moment. It's our kid, so you must have your love there too."

"I love you, that is really incredible. Let this be a proof of our love. The only issue will be finding a bisexual surrogate that agrees with the whole thing."

"Don't worry. Everything is possible. I will find one." They started to kiss. Eva pushed Chris flat on his back and started to kiss his chest, then his belly, always going down. They had a great morning of love they would never forget.

Some months later, Eva was traveling in San Francisco, and so she and Chris had their usual update discussion on the phone.

Then Chris said, "My love, I found a surrogate that has agreed to meet us. If we pass muster, she is willing to carry our child. I will send you some pictures, a DNA report, and some words she wrote about herself. If you are OK with it, we will meet her this weekend to get acquainted."

"Oh, that is great! Our kid project is starting," said Eva.

That Saturday they met Ashley, a very nice, brown-haired, white woman. She was very nice, and she seemed to be right for the job.

"Hi, Ashley, very nice to meet you. Please tell me something about you," said Eva.

"Well, I am from Wisconsin, have been living in Florida for about five years, and let's say I could use some cash. I am lesbian, but I can have sex with a man. Anyway, Chris asked me if you could be present and active during the insemination. Well, that's fine. I would prefer it if you were there because, I must be honest, being alone with a man is not exactly something I am used to."

They talked for quite a while, and finally, Eva said, "I think we will get along very well. I am OK with you." Chris gave his OK as well.

"OK, great. I propose that we sign the papers with the lawyer and just get down to it," said Ashley.

Well the formalities were over, and then they had to wait for Ashley to be ovulating. When that happened, they met for a very special evening. Ashley came to their home, they had a nice dinner, and it was clear that Ashley had clearly a better relationship with Eva than with Chris. They both started to kiss and caress her. Eva was massaging her and making her excited while Chris was kissing Eva all over her body. It was clear somehow that Ashley was ready, so Eva turned her attentions to her husband to make him very excited orally. It didn't take long for Chris to climax inside of her. They all made sure that Ashley was very relaxed before they stopped.

One month later they got a text from their surrogate: "Great news, I am pregnant. Well, not sure if great because I really enjoyed the evening, could get used to it."

Some months later Eva went with Ashley to the doctor where he gave her an ultrasound. It was clear that the kid had a penis, so probably it would be a man. The nine months of pregnancy came to an end, both Eva and Chris were present at the birth, and it was a very intense moment when that little human being came out of its natural mother and just cried. They called him Tylor, a gender-neutral name.

At that point it was clear, Eva had a new life, a new beginning, Chris had a child, and Eva was a mother now. After all these years, these changes, the different genders, lovers, and lives, now all was going to change.